dodging TEMPTATION

dodging TEMPTATION

AVERY FLYNN

Entangled Publishing, LLC
10940 S Parker Rd
Suite 327
Parker, CO 80134
rights@entangledpublishing.com

Indulgence is an imprint of Entangled Publishing, LLC.

Edited by Alethea Spiridon Hopson
Cover design by Elizabeth Turner Stokes
Cover photography by Luis Louro and CURAphotography/
Shutterstock

Manufactured in the United States of America

First Edition September 2015

Chapter One

Five miles into an eight-mile short run and Dodge Loving had hit his stride. Nothing could touch him right now. Not his younger brothers who were driving him nuts. Not his mom who meddled in everyone's life. And definitely not the anvil-heavy worry about every fucking thing that could go wrong at The Retreat Spa and Resort that weighed down his shoulders most days.

It was too early in spring for the Wyoming sun to be set to scorching, but still he'd soaked through his wicking T-shirt and shorts. Small clouds of dust puffed up around his feet as he rounded the dirt path's bend. The Retreat's main lodge loomed up ahead. Large, imposing, and made from foundation to roof of locally quarried stones and timber, it was a log cabin on steroids. It stood in the middle of nowhere in Wyoming with its own private access roads, landing strip, and helicopter pad. When the rich from either coast wanted to get away from it all, The Retreat was their first choice for a reason.

Privacy. Luxury. Freedom.

That's what The Retreat promised and what Dodge made sure each guest received, especially Garth Hampton. The aging rock star had arrived last night from his latest stint in rehab looking like death warmed over and reeking of desperation. Dodge had set him up in a private cabin half a mile from the main lodge. Glancing over his left shoulder as his feet thumped against the earth in time with his controlled heartbeat, he could see the cabin's roof behind the tree line. Like everything else at The Retreat, the cabin was a fifteen on a ten-point luxury scale.

The sun reflected off something in his peripheral vision. The sixth sense for trouble he'd developed running roughshod over his brothers stabbed a path up his spine. Knowing better than to ignore it, he paused his stride, took in a few deep breaths, stretched as if he was ready for his cool down, and covertly surveyed the area. All that stood between the resort's running path and the private landing strip were wildflowers in full spring bloom, a few trees, several bushes, and the occasional tumbleweed, nothing that could explain the glint of light.

Glancing up at the main lodge, he brought his right arm across his chest until his shoulder muscles protested. Pivoting on his heel, he switched stretching arms and turned so he was facing the landing strip. That's when he saw it again. The sun reflected off something in one of the bushes next to the path. Dodge sprinted over fast enough to scatter a couple of quail to the sky and reached through the branches. Greasy hair. Pasty skin. Creepy vibe. It only took a second to realize he'd caught himself a trespasser of the worst kind.

Fucking paparazzi.

He wrapped his fingers around the camera strap curled around the guy's neck and yanked him to his feet.

"The fuck, man?" The man tried to wriggle free.

In response, Dodge tightened his grip and pulled until

only the man's tiptoes touched the ground. With his telephoto lens, ketchup-stained T-shirt, and three-day beard, it wasn't hard to guess the guy's occupation. It didn't happen every day, but paparazzi snuck in often enough, trying to grab a million dollar shot of one of The Retreat's guests, that spotting the vermin at a glance—or first grasp—had become second nature.

"This is private property," Dodge said.

"Oh come on." The photographer's eyes bugged out a little. "I'm just doing my job."

In violation of the "No Trespassing" signs posted liberally around the perimeter. "Spying on The Retreat's guests?"

The man reached into his bramble-covered pants and pulled a twenty out of his pocket. "Look, take this and walk away. No one needs to know."

Like too many idiots, this guy assumed Dodge wasn't in charge. Was it because he was only thirty? Because his skin was about twelve shades darker than the vast majority of people in Wyoming? Could it be the sweat-soaked running shorts? Whatever the reason, Dodge didn't care. He'd play along to find out what the jerkwad wanted and kick him out on his fat ass. He plucked the money from the other man's fingers. "So who are you poking around looking for?"

If the press knew Garth Hampton had gone straight from rehab to The Retreat to write his next album, the shit would hit the fan. The Retreat was known for protecting the privacy of its ultra-rich guests. He couldn't let that track record get dinged or the deal with The Brasch Group to take The Retreat global with locations in some of the hottest vacation spots in the world would fall through, along with his efforts to ruin his bastard of a grandfather's hotel chain.

Jonathan Kerry owned a lot of businesses, but it had all started with the hotels, and they were what he cared about the most. Times were tough, though, and his grandfather's hotels were barely hanging on; they were desperate for an influx of cash from The Brasch Group. One they weren't going to get. Dodge couldn't wait to see the results of a year's worth of wheeling and dealing that would result in Kerry Holding Unlimited's hotels going belly up. It was past time the old man paid his debt, and Dodge was determined to collect.

"What business is it of yours why I'm looking around?" the paparazzi asked.

Bravado didn't go far when your feet were barely touching the ground. Dodge tightened his grip, and the man sucked in a wheezy breath as he clawed ineffectually at Dodge's fingers.

"Fine!" he managed to get out.

Dodge dropped him to his feet and waited. It didn't take long.

"Harper Conners." The photographer rubbed the back of his neck where the tightened camera strap had rubbed his skin raw.

He knew The Retreat's guest list like his youngest brother knew supermodels' dimensions. The name didn't ring any bells. "Who?"

"Damn, I really am in the sticks. Her family has more money than Midas, and she slapped her cheating senator husband silly on national TV during one of those mea culpa press conferences about eight months back. Ring any bells? How about the leaked audio of her leaving the best I'm-going-to-make-your-life-miserable-if-you-don't-sign-the-quickie-divorce-papers-now voicemail on her husband's cell phone? It's only played on every cable news outlet from here to Timbuktu for the past month. Come on, chief, you can't be totally clueless."

A vague memory shook loose. Red hair, big brown eyes, and an ass that made men do stupid, stupid shit without ever wondering why. "She's not here, so you best be on your way before I call in security."

The man rolled his eyes and adjusted the camera strap around his neck. "No offense, chief, but I know my job. She's here working as some sort of consultant."

Relief loosened his shoulders. Since he did all the hiring and firing at The Retreat, he'd know of any consultant on staff. "Wrong."

"Check it out." The photographer pushed a few buttons on his phone and brought up an email.

Certain phrases stuck out: *The Retreat Spa and Resort, rare cowboy diaries, book auction, May Loving.* His stomach lining evaporated. His mother had hired her. Of course she had. Why should this surprise him? "Shit."

"And the tabloids are willing to pay top dollar for any photos as long as it's the exclusive first get." The paparazzi leaned in and lowered his voice. "I can squeeze a few bills in it for you if you can get me closer. If someone gets it before me, all deals are off. It's only money if it's the first."

What a moron. "You won't believe how close I can get you." Dodge pressed the Bluetooth button on his smart watch with one hand and grabbed the photographer's upper arm with the other.

"Security," The Retreat's head of security answered.

"Hey, Frank. Meet me on the running path east of the main lodge. I got a snooper."

"On my way, boss."

The smug, hey-bro grin slid off the man's face like sloppy wet eggs off a plate. "Boss?"

"Dodge Loving, president of The Retreat and despiser of low-life paparazzi." He tightened his grip on the man's arm and smiled. It was about a hundred degrees colder than the aw-shucks grin he gave The Retreat's guests, and the photographer shivered in his tight grasp. "Can't say it's good to meet you, asshole."

• • •

If Harper Conner couldn't hide from the world in a library in the middle of nowhere in Wyoming and figure out how to become a new and improved version of herself, then she needed to hand in her ninja card—and she wasn't about to do that any time soon, at least not until the ink dried on her newly signed divorce papers.

So she'd work, plot, and plan in the library. Cataloging and authenticating the more than two hundred books in The Retreat's cowboy library could take a ton of time, but she'd only been hired for two weeks. It wasn't as long an escape as she wanted, but it still allowed plenty of time for the world to forget what a naive idiot she'd been, so when she went back to Washington they'd see her as the tougher, ballsier version she'd become. Not that everyone would accept the new her, which she knew from the near daily reminders from her mother, who never met a blatant spousal infidelity she could ignore.

But alone with the musty scent of old books and the light filtering in from the floor-to-ceiling windows at The Retreat's library, Harper could escape and plan her transformation. Books had always been her safe haven, and the job offer from May Loving couldn't have come at a better time. She settled into her chair, several tall stacks of books hiding her from view, and she eased open a small leather-bound journal. The writing was faded and cramped with a few girlish curlicues that gave away the writer's gender, if not her devilish nature.

Belle Starr had earned her nickname The Bandit Queen. She'd rustled cattle, stolen horses, and bootlegged whiskey on the western frontier, thumbing her nose at authority for years before dying in an ambush, killed by her own double-barreled shotgun.

"Ain't life a bitch?" she muttered to herself.

"You have no idea," a male voice said from the other side of the stacks.

Harper's surprised yelp bounced off the high ceiling, and her heart slammed against her ribcage as she jumped up from her chair. A man stood just inside the library's door. Tall—at least six-foot-four—he had warm brown skin, thick muscles, a movie star face and moss green eyes that sent a jolt of electricity beaming straight down to the center of her cherry red panties. He'd scared the bejesus out of her, but that didn't account for the awareness keeping her feet nailed to the ground. Sweaty, in running clothes, and more than a little bit pissed off, he had an aura of power and danger that twisted girls up and left them begging for more. Harper inhaled a shaky breath. She might need to sit down.

"I'm Dodge Loving." He stalked forward, all business. "Are you Harper Conner?"

That name sounded vaguely familiar. *Because it's your name, Harp. Pull it together.* "Yes."

He hesitated, seemingly searching for words on the wide hardwood planks that made up the floor, before raising his head and straightening his spine. "You're fired."

"What!" Her knees gave out, and she plopped down into the chair. Thank God she had plenty of padding on her ass, or the force of her crash landing might have broken her tailbone.

"You're on the first flight out tomorrow. We'll arrange for a car to take you there right away." He peeked over her book wall. "How quickly can you be packed?"

His blasé attitude cut through her shock. Pretty boy, mean attitude, wasn't that just her luck? Why did everyone assume she'd just kowtow to any and every authority figure? Sure, she'd spent her entire life up until six months ago with her toes planted firmly on the company line, but she'd crossed it, big time, and she wasn't going back. She'd made up her mind to take a strategic retreat from public life to learn how to become the new Harper, and this job, getting to do what she loved, was about as perfect for that purpose as possible.

With greater difficulty than she liked, she ignored her all too keen awareness of Dodge and leveled a glare at him that had silenced even the toughest bully at boarding school. "You can't fire me. Your mother hired me."

Her death look had absolutely no effect on Dodge, probably because he never looked up from his smartphone to see it. "She has nothing to do with The Retreat's daily operations. She should have told you that."

A loophole! "I'm not here on The Retreat's behalf. She hired me to authenticate and catalog her private collection of cowboy books for possible auction. You can't fire me, only she can."

He opened and shut his mouth several times.

"You being here isn't going to work." Dodge paced in front of the desk, so tall she had no trouble watching him above the stack of books. "Do you know what I found in the bushes?"

Harper crossed her fingers under the desk. "Quail?"

He rolled his eyes. "No. A slimeball photographer intent on getting photos of you."

Probably the same one who'd hacked her email right after her divorce became final last month. Why couldn't people just leave her the hell alone? "I assume you got rid of him."

That stopped him in his tracks. "Of course." He said it as if the universe wouldn't even allow another possibility.

Dodge Loving might be a Type A asshole, but in this instance he was *her* Type A asshole. She'd hated dealing with the press since the first time her mother had dressed her in something frilly and itchy before her dad plopped her down in front of the cameras for his failed presidential run. That her dad hadn't become president that time, or the next time he'd run, didn't lessen the press attention on her family, and they'd crowned her as some sort of political princess. Add to that the fiasco from eight months ago and the slap heard around the world...and yeah, she'd rather eat her own arm off than talk to the press. The fact that Dodge had gotten rid of one of the slimy bastards made her almost like him despite the fact that he was trying to fire her. She relaxed in her chair. "Thank you."

It hadn't been easy getting this job, and she wasn't giving up on it now. She'd been on six interviews before the offer from May Loving dropped in her lap. No one else in the conservative rare book field wanted to hire the woman whose name had become shorthand for a pissed off scorned political wife with a vendetta, but May hadn't cared. She'd said something about the universe having a plan, and that was that. Harper had gone to the airport and found the Loving family jet ready to whisk her off to The Retreat.

"You still need to go." Dodge continued to tap away on his phone. "He said there'd be more bottom-feeding reporters coming and we can't have that here. Our guests require utmost privacy."

And there probably would be more. Paparazzi replicated like gremlins after midnight. "Good thing I have all of these books here to keep me busy and indoors away from prying eyes or telephoto lenses—and you, of course, to watch out for me."

He kept tapping away on his phone, obviously confident she'd bend to his will. "If you're going to stay here, then you'll need to do an interview so they'll stop lurking around the place."

Her stomach lurched. "Absolutely not." The ironclad employment contract she'd signed clearly stated she'd lose her job if she did any interviews. Her boss, Simon, at Graveson Brothers Books, was militant that she bring no negative attention to the firm because of her past and, unlike what most people seemed to think, she didn't have millions tucked away in her bank account. Hell, she barely had a thousand dollars in her quickly dwindling savings account. And her boss all but promised that even a whisper of scandal and her employer's parent company, the Boston-based Kerry Holdings Unlimited, would use all of its many corporate attorneys to rain hell down upon her until she drowned. She couldn't afford to lose this job.

His head snapped up and he palmed his phone before going perfectly still. His muscular chest didn't even rise with his breath. The pompous ass had probably trained his organs to obey his every mental order. Five seconds. Ten seconds. Thirty seconds. She wasn't going to yield, but that didn't mean she wasn't going to squirm. Beads of nervous sweat gathered at the nape of her neck. Belle's diary wavered in her hand. She gulped down the urge to acquiesce. Old habits die hard, but she was determined to kill that one until it was dead.

Dodge's mossy green eyes had turned the color of emeralds. "You don't have a choice. In fact, I'll do whatever it takes to make sure of that."

Someone *really* didn't like having his plans spoiled. He glowered at her when she didn't immediately snap back in line. She straightened up in her chair. Being a badass was kind of fun.

"I always have a choice." That hadn't been the case forever, but she did now. She'd retired her political princess crown and squashed her knee-jerk reaction to always be the dutiful daughter and wife who did what was best to get a boost in the polls or ensure a vote—no matter what she really wanted. "If that's all you wanted, I have a lot of work to do."

He loomed over her, making the desk between them feel like as much of a barrier as a mini Lego. "All I want is for you to do an interview so the opportunity for an exclusive disappears and the jackals stay off my property."

"It's good to want things." Powered by bravado and a stubborn streak three miles wide, she winked. "It keeps you hungry." Without waiting for a response, she opened Belle Starr's journal back up to the first page, studiously ignoring the big bad wolf with too much testosterone glaring at her from less than two feet away.

He could huff and he could puff, but it was going to take a lot more than a hot guy with a stick up his ass to make Harper change her mind.

Chapter Two

The dark, musky patchouli scent hit Harper as soon as she turned the corner and entered the back hallway leading to May's meditation room. Set back from the public places in the thirty-bedroom main lodge, it was part of the original homestead. The walls were lined with warm oak, and large wood beams decorated the ceiling. It looked about as rustic and old school Wyoming as she could imagine. But as soon as she turned the crystal doorknob and entered the meditation room, it was like entering a new world.

The basic elements were the same, with wood covering every surface from floor to ceiling, but May had layered rich fabrics in autumnal colors over the plush armchairs and overstuffed cushions. Cream curtains hung from rods attached to the ceiling, separating one meditation space from another. Burning candles were scattered throughout the room, spreading the scent of patchouli and sandalwood, while the low thrum of chanting Tibetan monks played quietly over hidden speakers.

Harper searched the room for May and came to a

complete standstill as soon as she spotted her. The Loving family matriarch sat in the center of the room atop a chestnut-colored cushion, a look of total peace on her face that relaxed the crow's feet around her bright green eyes and melted the deep laugh lines that bracketed her mouth. Definitely not the time to bust in and rat out her employer's eldest son for trying to fire her.

Afraid to even let go of a breath and disturb May, Harper tiptoed backward, pulling the door shut as she went. The door was nearly closed when the heel of her cute kitten-heeled shoes caught on a groove in the wood, knocking her off balance.

Oh, sh—

She let out an involuntary squeal. Her head went back as her feet went straight up. The room tilted, and she landed with a hard *thwack* against the hardwood floor, cracking her head against the wood and slamming all the air out of her lungs. Pain shot outward from the back of her head, and she clenched her eyes shut, keeping them that way until the agony subsided. Her lungs began to function again, and she decided she wasn't going to die of anything other than embarrassment.

"Never go backward when the universe wants you to move forward," May said somewhere off to her left.

Harper blinked her eyes open and gingerly sat up. "That's one way to explain being a total klutz."

May laughed and sat down cross-legged on the floor beside Harper. "It's Dodge, isn't it?"

"What makes you say that?" Harper asked as she rubbed the sore spot on her head.

"A mother knows." Her lips curled up, but the Zen-like calm remained in her green eyes. "Plus I happened to be walking by the library when he tried to fire you."

Imagining what the scene must have sounded like echoing out into the hall, Harper flinched. To never cause a scene had been firmly implanted in her by her parents for whom image wasn't the most important thing—it was the only thing. Still, May could have stopped in to the library and set Dodge straight. "And you didn't tell him he couldn't do that?"

"Does one tell the river not to flow?" She shook her head, the movement making her dangling gold earrings sway and jangle. "Dodge is Dodge. He always has been wound up too tight. One of these days he's going to pop a spring if he doesn't find the right woman to unwind him."

"I feel sorry for her already." The words tumbled out before Harper could stop them. She cringed and fisted her hands by her side to keep from slapping her hand over her mouth. Insulting her biggest—and only—client's son wasn't the way to hold on to the job she needed. "Sorry, May, I..."

The older woman giggled, a light airy sound as fluttery as the gauze curtains hanging in the meditation room. "Don't worry about it. Dodge has that effect on some people."

"So will you talk to him? When I did, I just seemed to get under his skin and tick him off."

"I will." May cocked her head and gave Harper a considering look. "I'll talk to him *all* about you."

Trouble. The gleam in May's eyes was an all-caps trouble-ahead warning that sent unease skittering down Harper's spine. "On second thought, maybe it's best if we let him be."

"Oh no. Talking to him about you is a *perfect* idea. Someone who gets under his skin is exactly what he needs." May tossed her hands up in the air and did a shimmy with her narrow hips. "I should have realized as soon as I saw you and that flaming hair of yours that you'd light a fire in him."

That was one way to describe it. Still, Harper couldn't shake the feeling that May was plotting. If she'd learned anything growing up it was all about parental manipulation. "I'm not sure I like where this is going."

"The universe is like that sometimes, but we all end up

where we need to be and with whom we need to be." May gave her an assessing look. "Yes, the more I think about it the more I realize the universe has brought you here for a reason."

"To authenticate your cowboy diaries."

"No darling, to fall in love."

Oh no. Nope. No way. That was not going to happen, not anytime soon and possibly not ever again. She was done with love in all its manipulative forms. "The ink on my divorce is barely dry. The last thing I want is to make a love connection."

"Want and need are two totally different things." May shrugged. "You have to open yourself up to all the universe has to offer."

"Unless it's offering calorie-free ice cream, I'll have to decline."

"You sound just like Dodge, thinking you can force the universe into behaving. That's exactly why you're perfect."

Unease transformed into downright panic that made her palms clammy and her pulse jackrabbit. "I'm not sure—"

"That's okay, I'm sure enough for both of us." May rubbed the flat stone pendant she always wore and glanced up at the ceiling. "I got this one, universe."

She looked around. Yep. They were definitely still alone. "What do you have?"

"The solution to Dodge." The Loving matriarch beamed at Harper. "You."

Okay, this had officially landed her in the center of the crazy trail. "I don't think that's in my realm of expertise."

"It's time you begin to see beyond the expected." She curled her deceptively strong fingers around Harper's wrist and held tight. "It's scary, I know. When I met the boys' father, Hale, he couldn't have been more unlike what I was used to than if I'd put orange juice in my cornflakes. A Boston Brahmin heiress and the black cowboy from Wyoming." Her earrings jingled again when she ruefully shook her head. "My father disinherited me when I ran off with Hale, but I didn't care then, and I sure don't care now." She giggled her signature high-pitched trill. "A few months ago, I was at my weekly reading and Sarah Beth kept finding the love cards being tied in with the boys. That was clue number one. Then, when I was in Washington, D.C. and happened to run into you in the stacks at the Library of Congress? That was clue two. And now Dodge tries to fire you. That's three! How could I have been so dense to have missed it until now? Good things always happen in threes, and Dodge falling in love with you is a *very* good thing." May looked at Harper expectantly.

Harper tried to stop her eyes from bugging out. "That's not going to happen."

"The universe has plans for all of us."

"Well, this plan officially sucks, because I don't believe in love, especially not with a Type A CEO who thinks the whole world should jump when he snaps his fingers. I'm not the kind of girl who falls in love anymore." She whinged. Damn, she needed to start censoring herself when it came to Dodge Loving. "Sorry, I know he's your son."

The matriarch shrugged. "None of this is news to me, and that is exactly why you're perfect."

Backpedaling away from the meditation room hadn't worked so well the first time, but this whole situation was weird enough to make her try it again. She stood. "Thank you for the…ahem…offer, but I'm going to have to decline. I've got two weeks to catalog your rare cowboy diaries and books. It's going to take all my focus to get it done on time. The universe is going to have to find another girl for Dodge. Bye, May."

She spun on her heel and hustled down the hall before May could pull her any further down the crazy trail. Pausing at the wall of floor-to-ceiling windows in the walkway connecting the old homestead part of the lodge to the guest wing, she spotted Dodge and another man half hidden by a small grove of trees partway between the lodge and a private cabin set away from everything else. In comparison to Dodge's muscular runner's body, the other man looked like he'd been ridden hard and put up wet. Skinny, slouched, but still studly, he braced himself up with one hand pushed against the rough tree bark.

It took her a second, but there was no mistaking Garth Hampton. For the last thirty years he'd put out a string of number one albums and gotten rich. Rumor had it he was up for induction in the Rock and Roll Hall of Fame. The last she'd heard of the world famous rocker he was checking into rehab after an unfortunate incident with six groupies, a bottle of tequila, and an unexpected orgy on the el train in Chicago documented by paparazzi.

As if he could feel the weight of her stare, Dodge turned and his gaze caught hers. Her breath hitched, champagne bubbles bounced around her belly, and her focus dropped to the honey-brown floorboards before she tilted her chin just enough that she could watch him through her eyelashes.

Dodge said something to Garth who settled a baseball hat low on his head, hunched his shoulders up, and hustled off, staying as far away from any other person as possible. Looked like someone was here incognito. Her attention didn't stay on the aging rocker long, not with Dodge staring at her with the intensity of a man on the most important mission of his life. A shiver shook its way down her spine, turning her skin icy hot and puckering her nipples until they strained against the satin lining in her bra. His full lips curled into a cocky grin, as if he knew exactly the effect he had on her mutinous body, and she couldn't shake the feeling that she'd just been marked as prey.

. . .

The Retreat's ridiculously wealthy guests ate in the main lodge's exclusive dining room that looked like a rustic version of the top restaurants in New York, Paris, or Rome. Celebrity chefs rotated through the kitchen, bringing something new to the menu each month and keeping the foodie guests returning year after year just to see what was being served now.

The Loving family, though only slightly less wealthy than the people it catered to, spent most dinners together in the lodge's intimate private dining room. Dodge had always liked the separation. Even a Type A personality like him needed some downtime. But tonight wasn't about relaxing over steaks cooked to a medium rare perfection. It was about gathering intel on the woman whose very existence at The Retreat put his entire plan for his future in jeopardy.

Luxury, privacy, and total discretion, that's what The Brasch Group promised guests at all of its properties. All it would take was one paparazzi shot of Garth Hampton and The Brasch Group would pass over The Retreat and sign with his grandfather's hotels. That would be just the influx of cash the bastard of an old man needed to keep his hotels afloat. Dodge refused to let that happen.

The steak and baked potato were already waiting for him on a plate by the time he walked into the room. He pulled out a chair at the round cherrywood dining table between his brothers and sat down. Normal people would have scooted their chairs over a little bit to make room for him. His brothers were not normal people. They bracketed him in as tight as the cow chute at one of Stone's rodeos.

"Excuse me," he said.

"I've been trying to think up an excuse for you for years," said his youngest brother, Griff.

Stone didn't even look up from his plate piled high with

steak, potatoes, biscuits, broccoli drenched in cheese, and fresh shrimp flown in from the coast this morning.

Little brothers, would they ever learn? Probably not his.

Dodge planted his ass firmly in the chair and locked his thighs tight—they were his little brothers, but neither of them stood any less than six feet three. Stone spent most of his time wrestling bulls to the ground while most of Griff's wrestling happened behind the closed bedroom doors of Fremont, Wyoming's female population. One quick inhale and then on the exhale Dodge jammed his elbows into each of his brothers' ribs. The double *"oof"* they let out never got old.

"Boys." Warning lay thick in his dad's voice. "Cut the shit and scoot over. I swear to God, I have calves in the back pasture more mature than you three."

Their mother may be all about the touchy-feely call of the universe crap, but their father was pure Wyoming rancher. Hale Loving talked very little and took even less shit. The two were about as different as their skin tones, Hale as dark as a moonless night and May as light as The Retreat's porcelain serving dishes, but together they meshed. Someday he might have time for a life like theirs, but not until he'd built a financial empire to rival his grandfather's. The bastard had thrown May out when he'd discovered his daughter hadn't just fallen for someone outside of their tight social circle, but a cowboy from Wyoming whose large bank balance didn't negate the dark color of his skin.

"I had the most interesting conversation today in the meditation room with Harper," May said.

Dodge straightened in his chair, his pulse hammering a little quicker through his veins. What a total stroke of luck. For as quiet as his dad was, his mom loved to talk the way Griff loved to chase women.

"What about?" He took his first bite of steak.

She beamed at him. "The universe and how it's time for

you boys to marry."

Dodge choked on the steak lodged halfway down his esophagus. He gasped for air and the sanity that always seemed to elude him around his family. Stone's giant hand slapped him between the shoulder blades, hard enough to shake the Grand Tetons let alone clear Dodge's airway. He spit the mangled bite into his napkin.

"The universe doesn't get a say in any of that," Dodge said once he caught his breath.

"Whatever you say, sweetie. Just be sure to chew more carefully." May smiled and took another forkful of organic salad. She looked serene.

Dodge's palms turned sweaty, and he jiggled his knee under the table. His mom had the same at-peace-with-it-all look she'd had when she'd come to him before he left for college with an economy-sized box of condoms and a list of qualities that a girl would possess who would work well with his sexual aura. God love her, but boundaries weren't her thing. Cloaking her matchmaking tendencies in a bunch of new age buzzwords didn't hide her ultimate goal: marrying off her sons.

"I nominate Dodge to go first. He is the oldest." Griff smirked at him while maintaining enough distance to avoid another direct elbow shot to the ribs. "I hope this Harper chick is hot."

Only if a man went for that whole hourglass figure topped off with a model's face and intelligent chocolate-colored eyes. "I hadn't noticed."

Stone laughed. "Then you need to get your eyes checked, big brother."

Griff leaned forward and twisted so he was practically hanging over Dodge's dinner plate to get a better look at Stone. "Well, don't stop there. Details."

Dodge looked from one brother to the other, letting

his eyes tell them exactly what they could do with this little show of theirs. Some of this could be knocked up to giving him shit. However, it was also self-preservation. The more attention their mom focused on Dodge, the less she'd be trying to turn her matchmaking gaze on her other sons. If there were a zombie apocalypse, they'd lay down their lives for one another. But for one of their mother's matchmaking adventures? It was every brother for himself. If the tables were turned, he'd be doing the same damn thing. Shit, he had a million times already.

Stone tipped his chin toward the ceiling, no doubt trying to figure out how to describe the delectable Harper in front of their parents, before dropping his gaze back down to his plate. "Let's just say she hits his high points."

Griff moved his hands in the exaggerated shape of a Hollywood bombshell.

Stone nodded, a smile playing on his lips, but kept his attention focused on his fast disappearing steak and sides.

"I hope this one gives him a run for his money." Griff sighed dramatically. "He gets bored so easily."

They were laying it on thick. Whether the point was to get his mother's matchmaking juices flowing even more—if that was even possible—or to make him blow his top, he wasn't sure. It didn't matter, though, because neither was going to happen. There were more important things in his life than banging Harper Conner—like shoving success in the face of a wrinkled up racist relative. He sawed off a piece of his steak, using more force than was necessary, and the high-pitched screech of the knife on the ceramic plate betrayed his efforts to stay quiet.

"Careful there, brother," Griff said, giving him an ornery wink before addressing Stone. "Do you remember Shana?"

Stone let out a wolf whistle. "She was nice."

"Too nice." May shook her head as she stabbed another

forkful of salad. "No challenge there."

Dodge shoveled a piece of potato-covered steak into his mouth, grinding what had become a tasteless morsel into oblivion, and ignored his brothers. Well, as much as he could when they were bound and determined to take advantage of the moment to make his life hell.

"Whatever happened to Madison?" Stone asked. "She had fire."

"Just enough to dump his bossy ass." Griff demolished the last of his baked potato dripping in an unholy combination of ketchup and ranch dressing.

"I'm right here, you know." Dodge grumbled as he took another bite.

His brothers turned and said in unison, "We know."

Of course they did. It wouldn't be any fun if he wasn't. Bastards.

"What's Dodge's new girl's name, Mom?" Griff asked.

"She's not my girl." The protest shot out of his mouth louder and with more emphasis than he meant. Heat beat against his cheeks as frustration kicked his blood pressure up another twelve notches.

Griff shot him a shit-eating grin that plainly said he was enjoying every minute of his brother's misery. "Shh, don't interrupt your mother."

Ignoring her other sons, May zoned right in on Dodge as if she could will the match. "Harper is her name, and she is lovely."

"Lovely. Did you hear that, Griff?" Stone asked.

Griff nodded. "That translates into total babe, doesn't it?"

Stone took a long drink of water. "That would explain his interest."

Every man had his breaking point, and Dodge had arrived at the precipice—his hands had gone from sweaty to clammy, his back couldn't get any straighter if he had a fireplace poker up his ass, and a red haze had shaded his vision.

He slapped his palm against the table's unyielding surface. "My only interest is getting her out of here. With the paparazzi attention she brings with her because of her past it's only a matter of time before the press gets wind of Garth's presence. If that happens, we'll have a media shitstorm on our hands that will send The Brasch Group running as far away from us as possible. She brings the wrong kind of attention to The Resort." Not to mention the family dinner table.

"What past?" Stone and Griff asked at the same time.

Dodge pulled out his phone and punched up the YouTube video of the press conference Harper's then husband had held eight months ago. He'd watched it a million times already today. It started out as a typical politician-slept-around-and-got-caught press conference. Harper stood off to the side, even more pale than normal with a jaw so set he was surprised her teeth hadn't cracked. Yada, yada, yada from her senator husband about how he'd betrayed his family and the people of the great state of Vermont, and it was time for Dodge's favorite part. The bastard got down on one knee in front of Harper, held up a tiny blue tiffany box, and begged for her forgiveness. A flash of pure fury crossed her beautiful face for an instant before a serene mask fell into place. She looked down at the dumb bastard kneeling before her and whacked him with the mother of all bitch slaps right across the face. It nearly knocked him over. The gathered press went crazy, but Harper ignored them as she strutted out of the room.

Now that was a woman not to be messed with, just the kind he liked despite himself.

"Ouch." Griff rubbed his right cheek. "You might not want to piss her off."

"Or me," May said. "She's here at my request, and you're not to try to bully her away. She's in a delicate place in her life."

Dodge snorted. Harper was about as delicate as a briar patch made out of titanium.

"I ran into her the other night in the kitchen," Hale said. "That one is stress eating quarts of French vanilla during midnight fridge raids." A look passed between his parents, and Hale followed up in a rush with, "Not that there's anything wrong with that."

"It's better than her taking it out on his ugly mug." Griff nodded his chin toward Dodge.

He ate the comeback on the tip of his tongue. If he was going to find her weakness so he could exploit it and get her the hell away from The Retreat before the reporters sniffing around her picked up Garth Hampton's scent, there wasn't much of a better way to do it than to strike while she had the ice cream spoon halfway to her lips. Without meaning to, he imagined her mouth—all dewy and pink—and all the things he'd like to do with it. The list was long, lurid, and totally unobtainable. Harper Conner wasn't meant to be that kind of conquest for him. Tonight would be all about business.

Chapter Three

Mint chocolate chip was the only thing that would cure Harper's day. Rocky Road would work in a pinch, but only if it had actual chocolate pieces mixed in with the creamy goodness. She shuffled through The Retreat's empty, dimly lit kitchen in her PJs and bunny slippers, pausing long enough to swipe a spoon out of a drawer before continuing on to the walk-in freezer. It wasn't like she didn't have the route memorized by now. She should probably just get a mini-fridge in her room instead of storing her chocolate-dipped stress relief in here.

Food in her room…now that was something that would give her mother a conniption fit. Harper giggled as she imagined the look on her mother's Botoxed face and pulled open the freezer door.

"Looking for this?" A deep voice echoed off the restaurant-grade stainless steel appliances, making it sound as if it came from nowhere and everywhere at the same time.

Screaming like the banshee her father had often accused her of being after The Slap, Harper spun around to face the invader, holding the silver spoon over her head like a weapon.

The ice-cold wash of panic receded as quickly as it hit only to be replaced in an instant with an embarrassed flush.

Dodge Loving smirked at her and held out the small carton of Moose Tracks ice cream with her name scrawled across the lid in black marker. "Unless you wanted another flavor? You've got a collection going in there."

The old Harper would have slunk off to her room to listen to her stomach grumbling in private rather than be even the slightest bit embarrassed. It was amazing how slapping her lying, cheating, dirtbag of an ex-husband on national TV changed a woman. "Actually, I wanted the mint chocolate chip."

His gaze dipped down to the carton as if reading the name for the first time. "If you grab me a spoon, I'll swap out the cartons."

"Why?" He had an agenda—everyone always did when it came to her. Her parents had wanted a photogenic princess to parade in front of the press. Her ex-husband had wanted entry into the political elite. "You've already told me you want me gone so what's with the nicey-nice act?"

"Because you have good taste in ice cream." He shrugged his broad shoulders, pulling at the fine weave of his crisp white button-up shirt. "And because we got off on the wrong foot."

From his polished Italian leather shoes to his titanium cuff links—even at midnight, Dodge looked every bit like a man she should stay away from. Type A. All about control. Way too used to getting his way for his own good. Still, there was just enough Wild West in him to snag her attention anyway. Not that she planned on doing anything about it no matter what May Loving thought the universe wanted. The last thing in the world Harper needed or wanted was to fool around and fall in love—her new, most-unfavorite four-letter word. However, that didn't mean she should skip midnight ice cream. "I'll get you a spoon."

Twenty minutes and half a carton later they were facing each other as they sat on the stainless steel prep table in the middle of the kitchen with the carton of mint chocolate chip between them, each armed with a spoon. He'd ditched the shoes, rolled up his cuffs—revealing sinewy forearms that made her heart stutter—and told stories about how he ended up with the first name Dodge City.

"So all of you are named after old cowboy towns?" The idea of it was totally bizarre and endearing. Her being named Harper had scandalized her grandparents. Dodge City would have given them each a heart attack.

"Yep, my mother loves a theme." He shook his head and laughed. "Stone is short for Tombstone and Griff is short for Fort Griffin."

She scooped up a spoonful of ice cream, now melted more than when they'd started their midnight snack, and a line of green slipped over the edge. She stopped it with her finger before it could drip down to the table and licked the evidence off. "Did the other kids make fun of you growing up?"

When he didn't answer right away she looked up. His mossy green eyes had darkened, and his gaze was locked in on her mouth. A flush burned its way up from her toes, and she scrambled to think of something to say before her panties spontaneously combusted. "For your n-n-name…" She stumbled over the words. "Did they tease you about your name?"

He winked and smirked, all cocky confidence and testosterone-fueled sex appeal. "Only once."

If she could have gotten pregnant from a look, she'd be scheduling an appointment with her OB/GYN in the morning. Time to get out of this kitchen before the little seed of a romantic notion May Loving had planted took root and grew into the last thing Harper needed in her life right now. She'd spent her entire life up until eight months ago living by a script she'd never had any say in, let alone took part in writing. Neither the universe nor a my-way-or-the-highway hottie like the corporate cowboy here was taking her back there. She was her own woman now.

"You look like you're getting ready to wrestle a buffalo," he said.

"I hope not." Her denial came out far too soft and breathy for a woman only experiencing a sugar high.

"Then I'd suggest cleaning up a bit." Dodge swiped his thumb across the corner of her mouth—soft and slow, coming away with a dab of mint chocolate chip on his thumb, which he sucked off. "The buffalo around here have a real hankering for ice cream."

It took everything she had not to press her fingers to her tingling skin where he'd caressed her, as if her own touch could erase the sizzling sensation his had caused. It was only on that small space where her lips met, but it was the only thing she could feel. Her gaze held his, and her breath caught. There was no mistaking the want in his eyes. The air around them thickened, and words failed to materialize in her head.

Maybe it was the intimacy of the half-lit kitchen or the late hour, but she leaned forward over the carton between them without really meaning to. It wasn't much, an inch or two, but it was more than enough. He mirrored her move. Her eyes fluttered shut, and her lips parted in anticipation, then she detected a hint of icy mint before his warm lips covered hers.

· · ·

This was going to get messy, Dodge knew, but he'd been cleaning up other people's messes for most of his life. Why not take care of one of his own making for once, especially when the dilemma in question had some of the softest lips he'd ever wanted to kiss? Full to the point of pouty, Harpers's lips would tempt a saint standing in line at St. Peter's gate. So he gave in, leaned forward, and claimed the pink mouth of a woman who'd told him only a few hours ago to take a flying leap off a tall cliff.

It was heaven, hell, and purgatory all mixed into one dangerous sensation that turned his entire body into one hard divining rod for her. Balancing his weight on his palms pressed firmly into the prep table, he leaned toward her, deepening the kiss and sliding his tongue into her warm mouth. She moaned and twisted her tongue around his, teasing and tempting until he wanted to cede control to the insanity of the moment, pull down her ridiculous pink and green pajama pants, and take her right here on the prep table. His dick strained against his zipper, ready and willing to comply with the desire fogging Dodge's thinking. Hell, he wasn't thinking—that was the problem.

The bonging of the ten-foot high grandfather clock in the dining room reverberated through the otherwise silent kitchen, pulling him back to reality. Any other time, any other place, and that kiss wouldn't end now. He pulled back, missing the touch of her lips as soon as he lost contact. Not acceptable. He had to keep his eye on the problem at hand— namely Harper's unexpected camera-toting entourage—or risk losing everything he'd worked so hard for when the deal with The Brasch Group fell through. Losing focus or control wasn't an option, not at this point in the game.

"So..." She blushed, her cheeks turning the pink of dawn's first light. "It's getting late, and we both have to be up early tomorrow."

His mile-long to-do list scrolled through his head. Number one on it was ridding the surrounding Wyoming countryside of unsavory varmints with telephoto lenses. "So you know The Retreat guarantees its guests their privacy."

"That is one of the benefits of being out in the boonies,

no offense." She giggled, her face going from pink to red that nearly matched her hair.

"None taken." Unable to help himself, he curled a long strand of her hair around his finger, imagining it spread out on his brown chest or, better yet, feeling its silkiness against his thighs, before forcing himself to tuck it behind her ear. "That photographer I found snooping around said there would be more, and he's probably right. They won't stop coming until you give an interview."

She stiffened, transforming in a heartbeat from the woman he'd just kissed into the woman he'd tried to fire this morning—a spitfire sparking for a fight. "What about The Retreat's dedication to privacy?"

Okay, he was fucking this up royally. "You're not a guest, no offense." He laughed at his lame joke, hoping to regain at least a little of their earlier equilibrium.

Harper didn't even crack a smile. "Plenty taken." She shook her head and let out a chagrinned sigh. "Is that what that little kiss was about? You thought you'd slip me some tongue and soften me up until I agreed to do something you know damn well I'm not going to do?"

"That's not why I kissed you, and you know it." Heat blasted up from his toes at her accusation. Dodge straightened his cuff links and took in a deep breath before he lost his cool, something he rarely—if ever—did. Ruthless? Determined? An overall pain in the ass most times? He'd admit to all of that and more, but he wasn't a total douchebag. Rubbing his thumb over the titanium cowboy-boot cuff link like a talisman, he emptied the air from his lungs. "I can't fire you, but I can make your time here less than enjoyable."

"Is that a threat?" She crossed her arms, the move framing her generous tits and pressing her still hard nipples against the soft cotton of her BOOK NERD T-shirt.

He yanked his gaze back up to her face. "I don't have to

threaten people."

"Of course not." She smirked, her brown eyes narrowing to slits. "People naturally fall to their knees and genuflect when you walk by."

Now wouldn't that be nice? "I'll make the arrangements in the morning for the interview." He'd call Phil at *The Ledger* first thing. "I promise it will be painless."

"No you won't, because I know your secret." She stabbed her spoon into the half-empty ice cream carton like she was slicing into his heart.

He'd negotiated with tougher people than a woman who spent her days surrounded by stacks of dusty old books; her little bluff wasn't going to make him flinch. "Nice try."

Those pouty lips of hers curled into a Cheshire cat grin.

Shit. He hadn't just made a mess of the whole midnight ambush; he'd created a Superfund cleanup site. Fuck. She thought she had his balls in a vise with her bluff, but she couldn't be more wrong.

"I'm an open book, sweetheart." Now who was bluffing? "I don't have any secrets."

• • •

"Bullshit. If you don't back off this crazy plan of yours to force me into doing an interview, I'll reach out to every media outlet that will take my call and let them know that Garth Hampton is out of rehab and huddled up here at The Resort." Just making the threat made the ice cream curdle in her stomach. She'd never put someone through the hell of a media circus, not after living through it herself, but Dodge didn't know that. For her bluff to work, she had to make it seem like she was the kind of coldhearted bitch who'd do it. So, instead of taking back her words, she retrieved her spoon and pretended to savor her last bite of ice cream while he choked down her news. "Keeping that little tidbit secret is really why you want me to do the interview, isn't it?"

The vein in Dodge's temple bulged, and his nostrils flared. *Oops, looked like she pissed off the corporate cowboy. Whatever would she do now?* She smiled with enough fake sugar to give him a toothache—at least her time at debutant training had finally come in handy.

"That's blackmail," he said through clenched teeth.

"No. It's hardball, and I learned it at the feet of a master. My father didn't almost become president because he looks good on camera. It takes a hell of a lot more to claw your way to the top of that hill." And it was about time she put Daddy's unintentional lessons to use. She wasn't about to let Mr. Tall, Dark, and Bossy run her off when she didn't want to go. "I know your type, Dodge Loving. You're used to always getting your way. Well, that's not going to happen this time."

May Loving had hired her to do a job. She was good at that job. And she wasn't leaving until the job was done—plain and simple. She was so over getting pushed around by men in thousand dollar suits who thought she was their pawn to move around on a chessboard.

"I wouldn't bet on it," he said.

"Good thing I'm not a gambling kind of girl, otherwise you'd be out a good deal of cash." Harper hopped down from the table, placed her spoon into the dishwasher, and closed it with a firm click before strutting to the door. "Don't stay up too late frothing at the bit, Dodge. I'd be disappointed if you weren't at the top of your game tomorrow."

She sashayed out the door, making sure to give her hips a little bit of extra sway as she made her diva-worthy exist. Her entire body buzzed from an excitement that had nothing to do with a sugar rush and everything to do with her momentary victory over the man snarfing down the last of her mint chocolate chip.

Chapter Four

Cell phone glued to his ear, Dodge found his mother right where he knew she'd be at nine in the morning after leading a group of guests through a yoga session—on the family's private veranda with a cup of chai and a plate of flax seed muffins. May might be on the hippie- dippie side, but the woman loved a routine. It was the one thing they'd always been able to agree on. If anyone was going to understand the importance of getting back to their regular schedule, it would be her.

"You still there?" the Retreat's chief of operations, Randy Hayward, asked.

Dodge paused in the veranda's doorway and answered into his phone. "I'm here. You got rid of him?"

"I wish it had only been him." Hayward sighed, and his chair creaked repeatedly. That wasn't good. Dodge could picture the bowling ball of a man rocking in his well-padded office chair just like he did whenever a crisis approached. "We found a freelance reporter, a tabloid photographer, and a scout for a TV crew poking around by the front gates right as a shuttle was taking some guests into town to go antique shopping."

His ulcer woke up and said good morning, piercing his gut with a railroad spike. "All gone, I hope."

"Of course, but that's not all."

"What now?" It wasn't even lunch and he already needed a bottle of antacid, a whiskey neat, and a certain redheaded sexpot to get the hell away from his resort.

"Several of the guests are asking questions."

For a bunch of people who swore they valued their own privacy, they sure as hell loved snooping their way into everyone else's business. "About what?"

"Other guests, the staff, everything," Hayward said. "I think someone might be trading a little positive media exposure for themselves in exchange for a scoop about whomever we have here drawing all the media attention to The Retreat."

"Great." No matter the non-disclosure agreement each guest signed at check-in, gossip about one of the most famous rock stars in the past half century holing up post-rehab at The Retreat would be too good not to share—if they found out he was here. The media circus would go from one tent to twenty by nightfall. The Brasch Group would withdraw their financing offer, and his scumbag grandfather would reap the rewards of Dodge's failure.

Hayward cleared his throat. "And Mrs. Von der Gunston is checking out early. Said the place isn't up to her usual privacy standards. Others are starting to grumble. You know how guests are like sheep. We have to find a way to get rid of the press, or we're going to have more guests leaving or, even worse, someone finding out that you-know-who is here."

Like Dodge didn't know that. "I'm on it." He hung up, turned the phone to vibrate, and shoved it into his inside jacket pocket. The key to making a deal was knowing your partner's quirks. His mother hated cell phones, and he sure as hell didn't need an ill-timed ringing to put her off his plan to make things right.

The Brasch Group's representatives would be here in a few weeks for an in-person review and to sign the paperwork. By then, everything needed to be back to normal at The Retreat. He'd gone down in flames with Harper last night, but he hadn't given up. Not by a long shot.

"Good morning, darling." His mom held out a small purple plate. "Would you like a muffin?"

About as much as he wanted Harper to lead the press straight to Garth Hampton's cabin. "Thanks." He took the smallest bite possible, but the gritty dry whole wheat, flax, and God-knew-what-else concoction stuck to the top of his mouth like flavorless peanut butter.

"Chai?" She reached for her favorite teapot.

He choked down the muffin. "No, I'm good." There was no way he could have the muffin and the chai without his meat and potatoes stomach going into system failure as a protest. "I stopped by to ask a favor."

May settled back into the wicker chair's forest green cushion. "Anything, you know that."

He rested his ass against the stone railing so he faced her. His mother, with her hemp shirt and long braid, might look like a pushover, but he'd learned a long time ago that wasn't the case. The woman had a spine as hard as the porch railing and hated it when people beat around the bush. Time to go straight at it.

"The press is hanging around here like hungry jackals trying to get an exclusive photo of Harper or, even better, an exclusive interview," he said. "I need you to get her to do an interview so the press will back off."

"And you think one interview and photo shoot will get them to go away?"

"Yes. The tabloids are only paying out for the first exclusive. After that, it's old news."

"Since that's the case, why don't you ask her to do the interview?" May asked.

"I have. She said no." This is where he should have added in Harper's turn at blackmail, but something held him back. He needed his mother's help, not for her to go all mama bear and push Harper even further into a corner.

May shrugged and took a sip of chai. "Well, that's that."

"You don't understand." He pushed off the railing and paced the short length of the porch, each step winding the tension tighter instead of releasing it. "The longer the press sneaks around here trying to get a photo or surprise quote from Harper, the more likely they are to discover that Garth Hampton is here."

"And he wouldn't like that?" May took another sip of chai as if that discovery wouldn't have far-reaching effects on The Retreat, his plans for expansion, and his plot for revenge.

"Not in the least. He's a fifty-year-old recovering alcoholic who just got out of rehab. The last thing he needs is the stress of dealing with the press right now. He asked for total privacy, and I guaranteed it." He didn't go back on his word. Ever.

May cocked her head to the side and gave him a considering look. "There's more."

"Guests are already talking, and some have checked out." He rubbed the back of his neck, trying to ease the tightness there. "Plus, The Brasch Group's team is headed here in a few weeks to finalize the expansion agreement. If they get here and see a reporter hiding in the bushes and news vans parked between the tumbleweeds, the deal will go south faster than Stone got bucked off his last bronco."

"And you think all the reporters will disappear once Harper talks to them."

"It's a busy news cycle," he said as he stopped pacing and turned to face his mom. "They'll be gunning for the next big exclusive."

Quick, easy, and efficient, an interview was the best solution to fixing a shitty situation before it got worse. His mother had to see it. Looking into her eyes, the same shade as his own, he saw understanding dawn. Tension ebbed out of his upper back, and he rolled his neck with relief.

"The universe is giving you an amazing opportunity here with Harper coming into your life." May sat her empty mug down on the side table and clasped her hands together. "She's what you need, so stop trying to piss her off and find another solution to your reporter problem."

His ulcer threatened to rip a hole right through his stomach, and his chest tightened. Fisting his hands at his side, Dodge clenched his jaw shut and inhaled a deep breath. He had to figure out what the hell his mother was talking about and why the universe according to May always seemed to fuck with his plans. Then he could clean up this mess. The fresh Wyoming air filled his lungs, and he focused on the smell of freshly mowed grass, a reminder that the deal to take The Retreat global wasn't falling apart around them. Yet.

Releasing the breath, he forced calmness into his tone that he was far from feeling. "I don't want the universe's help."

May shook her head, her straight posture melting into a slumped *C*. "No, you just want your revenge."

That cut his bluster off at the knees. "You know about that?"

He'd never told her about his plans to pay his grandfather back for the way he'd tossed his own daughter aside. Showing the twisted old fuck that they didn't need him—would never need him—had fired Dodge's drive since he was sixteen and had found the letter the bastard had written May. Cold, cruel, and concise, the letter outlined exactly why his grandfather was disowning his daughter. For a sixteen-year-old trying to understand who he was and where he was going, that letter provided all the direction an ambitious teenager needed. At that age, nothing felt as good as telling The Man to fuck off.

"I'm your mother, so there's not a whole lot I don't know about you, Dodge." She stood, crossed the porch to him, and gave his shoulders a quick squeeze. "While I appreciate you wanting to right the wrongs done to me, you don't have to. I made my peace with my father and what he did a long time ago. The longer you hold on to this grudge, the more it will cloud your vision until you can't see all the good things that are right in front of you, or in the library for that matter."

"I can't forget or forgive."

May sighed and pointed to the newly planted cottonwood trees that in a few years would grow big enough to provide a little privacy for the family's veranda. "Just look at those saplings. If they don't bend to the never-ending Wyoming wind then they'll snap in half before they ever get a chance to grow into strong trees." She poked him in the ribs. "You have to learn to bend a little, Dodge, or you'll break."

That wasn't going to happen. He'd bend the rest of the world first—starting with Harper. He just needed to find out what button to push to make her agree to the interview. Maybe he could wheedle some information out of her employer.

"What company did you say Harper worked for?"

May averted her gaze. "I didn't."

Dodge's trouble detector went into overdrive. "Why?"

May's sigh was long and deep, the kind that alerted the world that bad news was coming. "Because your grandfather owns the company, and I knew it would only upset you."

Heat blasted through, temporarily blinding him to anything but his long-nourished hatred of his grandfather. Did the old man know about Dodge's plans for The Brasch

Group? Had he sent in a spy? The bastard would do it.

"What were you thinking?" Harsh and cold, he flung each word like a dagger.

May didn't flinch. She raised her chin and gave him *the look* every kid knows too well. "That she was the best person for the job."

"But she works for *him*." She had to be a spy. How much had she learned about their operations already? The Brasch Group representatives would be here soon. Was she planning sabotage?

May patted his cheek, a sad understanding softening her momentary hard edge. "You have got to let this grudge go before it eats you up."

Dodge didn't say anything. He couldn't. He was too busy figuring out how to use this information to force her hand about the interview before kicking her sweet ass off his property.

"Well, I'll leave you to your stewing." May gathered up her cup and the muffin plate before walking to the door. "I have a yoga class in fifteen."

He didn't stew. He plotted. He planned. He—

Harper, accompanied by Griff, walked into his line of sight and destroyed every other thought in his head. Faded jeans had never looked as good as they did hugging her full hips and high, round ass. She laughed at something his brother said, and the soft sound carried across the air, taunting him with its easy joy when he knew damn well there was nothing easy about her.

Stubborn, determined, and more than willing to fight dirty, Harper had gotten under his skin. That didn't happen often, if ever. He needed to go inside and figure out what his next step should be, but he couldn't leave the railing, not while the sun turned her auburn hair into a fiery gold halo around her. Good thing he knew she wasn't anywhere near as angelic as she looked, otherwise he'd be in trouble.

She spotted him watching, and a flash of heat sizzled between them, making his zipper work overtime. Insta-hard didn't even begin to describe it. The woman was probably a corporate spy who was blackmailing him and she still gave him a hard-on. That wasn't right.

Her step faltered the tiniest bit, and Griff grabbed her elbow before she lost her balance. Turning her head, she said something to him that Dodge couldn't hear, but she must have thanked him, judging by how his younger brother gave his best aw-shucks smile and tipped his cowboy hat. He didn't let go of her arm as they walked around the corner and out of sight.

There was no reason for Griff to have kept touching her like that. Harper was more than capable of walking on her own, not that he cared if she fell into his little brother's bed, but it could cause more problems. Office romances got messy fast, especially when it came to Griff, who wasn't known for staying tangled in the same sheets for long. Dodge's gut tightened, and the hip-high stone wall bit into the palms of his hands. Fuck it. If she wanted his brother, he wouldn't stand in her way. Maybe Griff could get her to agree to the interview, and Dodge could have the pleasure of banning her from The Retreat. Then everyone would be happy, except for his bastard of a grandfather.

Dodge stomped across the veranda and yanked the door open hard enough that it hit the wall and nearly rebounded against his head. Maybe a hard whack was what he needed to get thoughts of Harper and her pouty lips out of his brain for good.

Chapter Five

A handful of late-night revelers spilled out of The Retreat's low-key wine bar and onto the wide front porch. From there they could see nearly every star, glimmering with almost searchlight brightness in the inky black Wyoming sky. Dodge's gaze skimmed the guests, looking for signs of discontent that needed to be smoothed over and spotted none. The relaxed faces of his guests should have set him at ease, but they didn't.

Everything about him was wound up as tight as a rubber band about to snap. Ready. Edgy. Revved up for action. He'd been like this since that woman had poked her head up above a stack of worn books in the library and told him she wasn't going to play things his way. He'd pushed, and she'd stood her ground. That didn't happen with him. His mother was wrong. He wasn't the tree. He was the wind, and people bent to his will, but not Harper. She'd thrown everything out of whack.

Loosening his jaw before he cracked a tooth, Dodge made his escape from the veranda before another guest in ten thousand dollars' worth of diamonds tried to wheedle information out of him about the reporters skulking outside the gates. He squinted his eyes against the harsh brightness of the two-story lobby compared to the easy darkness outside. Taking inventory as he walked, he took mental notes so he'd remember to congratulate the staff on managing to balance the luxury and rustic charm of what was really a top-of-the-line log cabin on steroids.

He should go straight up the grand staircase to the family quarters in the west wing, but swerved left around the steps without thinking too much about why. A minute later he sat inside The Retreat's dimly lit library, the side door of which would open up to a short staff hallway leading to the kitchen. He had a sudden craving for mint chocolate chip ice cream and a deceptive corporate spy with a great ass.

"Burning the midnight oil?" Griff peeled away from the library wall, a book in his hand and an ornery look on his face.

Dodge slowed to a stop. "Just got the munchies."

"How convenient. Harper passed through here on her way to the kitchen a few minutes ago." Griff snapped the book closed and slid it home on the bookshelf. "But then again, I expect you know that already."

He stiffened. "Is that why you're here after you spent the afternoon sniffing after her heels?" Try as he might, Dodge hadn't been able to get the image of the two of them together out of his head. It had eaten away at him, wrecking his peace of mind with each sharp bite. "That would explain why you're here. Don't think I've ever seen you in the library before."

Griff chuckled like his brother's dig hadn't even registered. "It's not really my kind of place, but Harper gave me some ideas, and I wanted to give them a whirl."

"What kind of ideas?" He knew the kind of ideas his brother usually had and The Retreat's library didn't have a copy of *The Kama Sutra*.

"Not the kind you're thinking of, although maybe I should

start there with her. With that nice round ass and those heavy tits of hers, she might be just the distraction I need."

An angry heat scorched Dodge from the inside out, but he held it together. Control was his best weapon when it came to brotherly love taps like this.

"You know she works for our grandfather. He probably sent her here to spy on us and sabotage the deal with The Brasch Group."

"She's not a corporate spy."

"Oh, she told you that? You're too trusting."

"And you're sounding more like our my-way-or-the-highway grandfather every day."

"Fuck you."

"Maybe that's what you need to get you off your high horse. A good fuck with a hot chick who doesn't think the sun rises and falls on your hairy ass." Griff arched his eyebrows. "What, no reaction? Damn, she is just business for you then, but then again isn't everything with you?" His brother shook his head and mumbled something under his breath that sounded a lot like "stupid asshole."

"Not everyone in this world is obsessed with chasing tail," he said.

"And that's where you fuck it up, brother." Griff grabbed a book off the shelf and winged it at Dodge.

He caught it without the slightest fumble. "Enlighten me."

"It's not about getting ass," Griff said. "It's about having fun with someone else, getting your rocks off, and everyone walking away happy. Not everything is an all-or-nothing, win-or-lose situation, dumbass. If you weren't so focused on making the next big deal you might realize that."

Griff couldn't be more wrong if he were a broken clock. Winning wasn't the best thing, it was the only thing. And the way for him to win was to be the final nail in his grandfather's

hotel business by having The Brasch Group choose The
Retreat instead of his grandfather's hotels. And to make that
happen, Harper had to bend to his will.

Unbidden, a mental image of a naked Harper over his
desk flashed in his mind along with a brilliant solution to all
his troubles. Conventional wisdom said to keep your friends
close and your enemies closer. Well, you couldn't get much
closer than what he pictured doing to Harper. Blackmailing
spy or not, she was a woman on the rebound, and he had
every intention of screwing her before she got a chance to
fuck him over. No one ever said business—or life—was fair.

"Don't hurt yourself looking up all the big words." Dodge
tossed the book back to his brother, turned on his heel, and
stormed out of the library and into the short hallway leading
to the kitchen.

Loosening his tie with one hand, he leaned his shoulder
against the swinging door and entered the kitchen. The light
over the industrial sink was on, and the walk-in freezer door
stood open. An off-key rendition of "All I Want for Christmas
is You" filtered out from the freezer. Harper. It had to be. He
paused mid-step, the first hint of a smile cracking through
his pissed off shell. The woman was horrible, a singing-in-
the-shower-couldn't-even-help level of awful. She might be
the only person in the world who could give him a run for his
money in the shitty singing category.

He released the breath pushing against his ribcage like
an overfilled balloon. Her caterwauling did more to unwind
the tension in his shoulders than the punishing workout
he'd put his body through this afternoon. He removed his
cowboy-boot cuff links, dropped them into his shirt pocket,
and rolled up his sleeves as he made his way to the freezer,
getting there in time for Harper's big finish.

Dressed in black yoga pants and a tank top that made his
mouth go sawdust dry, Harper sang her way to the front of the

freezer with her eyes closed and a spoon for a microphone. "All I want for Christmaaaaas is youuuuuuuuu."

When the note cracked, he broke in. "You know it's May, right?"

Harper's eye's snapped open, and the drawn out "you" turned into a startled yelp. Her singing was pitchy, but her scream was downright earsplitting. A deep flush raced up from her cleavage, turning the miles of creamy flesh nearly as red as her hair.

"Would you stop doing that?" Eyes narrowed and attitude set on kill, she stormed out of the freezer armed with her spoon and half a gallon of ice cream and kicked the door shut behind her.

"What?" He didn't bother hiding his grin. "Telling you the month?"

She stormed past him, giving him a wonderful view of her ass covered in the clingy black fabric, and headed for the hall door. "No, scaring the shit out of me."

"Sorry." He slipped in front of her, cutting off her escape route, and tapped on the frozen half gallon's lid. "What's the flavor tonight?"

"Cookie dough and, before you ask, no—I'm not sharing." But she didn't make any moves to circle around him. For as cold as her words were, everything else about her was fiery hot.

She nibbled on her bottom lip and the tension that had ebbed out of his muscles came back in full force. Last night her full lips had tasted of mint chocolate chip and temptation. Tonight, he wanted to taste more than the ice cream off her lips. He wanted to drown in her. Mixing business and pleasure was about to get interesting, but as long as he remembered who she worked for, he'd be the one coming out on top.

She smelled of lilacs, fresh soap, and the kind of trouble a man couldn't help but get tangled up with. Pink tinted her porcelain skin, the last reminder of her earlier flush. Her nipples tented the smooth fabric of her tank top. From the freezer or him? If it wasn't him, he sure as hell wanted his chance to show her what he could do.

Hard and hungry for her, Dodge stood his ground even as every urged him to take what he wanted—what she wanted. This wasn't a typical mutual seduction. He had to take it slow so he could find out exactly what she was planning with his grandfather and counteract it without either of them being the wiser. But, of course, that didn't mean he wasn't going to enjoy every minute of it.

"You're not sharing?" Instead of reaching for Harper, he toyed with the carton's lid, popping it open, his gaze never leaving hers. "Not even a spoonful?"

"No." She slapped her hand over his, shutting the ice cream lid. "You're on my shit list."

"That makes us even. You're on mine, too." He brought his thumb up, stroking it across the center of her soft palm, even that simplest of touch making his cock hard. "Half a spoonful and in exchange I'll provide the whipped cream and maraschino cherries…as long as you promise not to sing."

• • •

It was the whipped cream that pushed Harper over the edge into saying yes, not the tingling sensation traveling up from her palm when Dodge touched her or the slip-sliding warmth that settled low in her stomach every time she saw him. She sprayed a second shot onto her ice cream. Definitely the whipped cream.

She lifted the spoon, but her muscles locked when she glanced up. He was staring at her with enough hot lust in his green eyes to set off every alarm bell and oh-girl-get-out-now warning bell in her head. No one had ever looked at her like that before. Not her parent-approved boyfriends, not her ex-husband on their wedding day, not a single solitary soul. But Dodge did, and she liked it. Really liked it. Never-wanted-him-to-stop kind of liked it. And she didn't have time for that. Her timetable was clear. Two weeks to finish authenticating May Loving's library and then she was out of here and back to her real life on the East Coast—as messed up as it might be at the moment. She needed to concentrate on rebuilding her life, not adding more complications to it.

Holding out the spoonful of cookie dough ice cream topped with a dangerous level of whipped cream she asked, "You didn't poison it, did you?"

The tangible electricity sizzling between them lost some of its voltage at her snarky question, but it lingered below the surface.

"Damn, you figured out my plan so easily." Dodge twisted an imaginary mustache before adding five cherries to the three scoops in his bowl.

She devoured her bite and pointed her empty spoon at him. "I've learned the hard way about men like you," she said with mock seriousness.

"Yeah." He nodded. "I saw the video of your ex's press conference."

Now that brought the mood right down to shittastic levels, and all the sense of silly fun leaked out of the room like air from a damaged balloon. "You and most of the world."

Embarrassment beat against her cheeks as she carried her bowl over to the small, utilitarian table in the corner and sat down. The metal chair didn't offer any comfort or give, not that she needed or wanted any. As her mother had so succinctly told her when Harper had turned to her after the disastrous press conference, everyone loves to see all the ugly in someone else's life, and she'd just handed it to the masses on the silver spoon she'd been born with in her mouth. Harper had been raised to only show the pretty, and with one impulsive action had invited the world to see all the ugly. Now they'd never stop looking for more.

Dodge settled down across from her. "You have a hell of a slapping hand."

She'd felt that smack against her palm for fifteen minutes after she'd stormed off the dais while the reporters screamed questions at her back. The wide-eyed look of surprise on her ex's face the split second before her hand made contact had almost been worth it. Almost.

"He deserved it." She shouldn't say more, but something about sitting across from Dodge in a deserted kitchen in the middle of the night relaxed the always-keep-your-private-life-private lessons she'd learned growing up. The words unraveled from around a rock that had been taking up too much space in her gut since the press conference, weighing her down and making each step toward a new life more difficult than it should be. "I told him the only way I was going to that press conference as my final act as his wife was if I got to stay in the background, didn't have to say a damn thing, and that he'd agree to get a quiet divorce a few months later once the media started talking about other scandals. He decided to improvise with that melodramatic proposal."

Dodge chuckled. "And paid the price."

"Both of us have." She took a bite of tasteless cookie dough ice cream, and it melted on her tongue. "My family was less than thrilled. The daughter of a former presidential hopeful slapping her senator husband on live TV is frowned upon. Who knew?" Bitterness rose like bile, and she pushed the small bowl of ice cream away.

"So you became a book...person?"

She laughed. "A book appraiser. I authenticate rare books and put a value on them." It was the dream job she almost never got, thanks to the media attention from The

Slap. "The book appraisal and authentication world is even more conservative than the political world. It took me months to find anyone who would hire me. When I did, my boss made it very clear that if there was another splashy scandal, I'd be fired."

"But you have money; it's not like you need the job."

"Actually, I do." The mental image of her bank account made her groan. "My parents have more of an appearance of wealth than the real deal, so I can't go running to mommy and daddy even if I wanted to—and I turned down alimony." She shrugged. "So here I am, a working stiff who needs to keep her head down to keep her job and keep the electricity on."

He pointed at her bowl and raised his eyebrows in question. She shrugged.

Scooping up half melted ice cream from her bowl, Dodge shook his head. "See now, out here in Wyoming we would have given you a medal and probably a sizable monetary reward for that slap."

"I'll keep that in mind." She watched him demolish what was left of her ice cream, noticing for the first time the small scar splitting his right eyebrow in two. Unless he had some kind of *Fight Club* secret he kept well hidden, she'd bet money one of his brothers had given it to him. However, his take-control attitude, my-way-or-the-highway dominance, and lethal levels of hotness were all his, which is why the relaxed, go-with-the-flow Dodge sitting across from her had her looking for answers. "So what's with the nice act all of a sudden?"

He sat back in his chair and crossed his arms. "I'm always nice."

The slow, deliberate wink he gave her and the way her nipples peaked in response declared otherwise.

"No." She shifted in her seat and squeezed her thighs

together, trying to ease a need that only increased the more time she spent with Dodge. And yet she didn't get up and leave. It was like the string of attraction drawing them together was getting shorter and shorter, forcing them closer. "You're always bossy."

"But in a good way." The cocky grin on his face said that he knew all the ways it would be good.

Harper laughed. It was weak and a little breathy, but it was either that or turn into a puddle of want at his feet, and she wasn't about to do that. The kiss the other night had been bad enough, and it ended even worse. He wanted her, but he also wanted something from her, and she needed to remember that.

He stood up and circled around the table before sitting down on the corner next to her right elbow. "Can we start over?"

Holding fast to the last bits of sanity she could grasp, she scooted her chair back from the table, giving her a few blessed inches of air between them. God, the man was killing her. "I'm listening."

"Hi, I'm Dodge." He held out his hand.

She shook his hand, going for a quick release that did little to stop the uptick in her pulse and the shiver working its way up her spine. "Harper."

Glancing down at his hand as if he felt it, too, he squeezed his hand into a fist a few times before letting it drop casually to the table. "I'm going to be totally honest and up front here. I need your help, Harper."

"Go on." *Just listening to him wasn't bad. Right?*

"You know Garth Hampton is here at The Retreat as a super-secret guest."

As if that was news to her. "He needs to stay in his cabin if he wants to stay secret."

"Agreed." Dodge rubbed the spot where his neck met his

shoulder. With the sleeves of his expensive shirt rolled up, the move highlighted his well-muscled forearm. "I've talked to him about that, but if the reporters who've followed you here find out he's here, then his cover is blown. He just got out of rehab, and dealing with the press is about the last thing he wants to do."

"Now that I can understand." Just the idea of having to deal with the shouts and the rude questions again was enough to make her palms sweaty.

"So could you find it in you to do a short interview with a guaranteed friendly press contact of mine to get the jackals off the scent?" He held up a hand, silencing the "no" already on her lips. "It would be tastefully handled, no splashy scandal. It would be like you were putting out an old fire for good, and then the media would finally move on to other targets."

She twisted her napkin until it tore in two. "Even if I wanted to, which I don't, I can't. My boss was crystal clear. Any media attention and I lose my job."

"I have connections," he said. "I can help you find another job."

She should say no. Her head was screaming for that outcome, but her heart was whispering something else entirely. "I'll think about it."

"Really?" He looked as if he never thought his plan would work.

"Yes, I'll do that." Really, what would it hurt to consider it?

"Thank you."

She giggled at his slack-jawed surprise. "Don't make such a fuss about it. I better get back to my room. I have a date tomorrow with a cowboy diary." And if she stayed in here with him any longer, God knew what she'd agree to next. Remaining in the kitchen with him meant only one thing: temptation. Hot, sweaty temptation and she'd had about all she could take of dodging temptation for one night.

He stood up and gathered their empty bowls as if he didn't have an entire staff of people paid to clean up after him. "Let me walk you back to your room."

Following him across the kitchen, she paused outside the door. The urge to stay a few minutes longer made each step away feel like moving through fast-drying concrete. "I'm okay."

"You're in the east wing, right?" He put the dishes in the dishwasher. "We're going the same direction. We might as well go together."

When he put it that way... "Let's go."

The Retreat's main lodge had started out as a rich rancher's five-bedroom homestead and only gotten bigger after that. As they made their way from the kitchen to the lobby and up the stairs to the east wing, Dodge pointed out the bits of the original structure that remained. He explained the painstaking process his dad had undertaken to make the transition to the additions that tripled the size of the already large main lodge, throwing in plenty of local history to help her connect the dots about why May Loving would have so many first edition cowboy diaries. Most of the men and women who'd scrawled down their thoughts must have crossed through this part of Wyoming at one time or another. The walk to her room took less time than she wanted and probably more time than it should have. She wasn't sure whether to be thankful or curse the lack of people in the hallways at one in the morning.

"So this is my room." She pulled the key card out of the zippered pocket on the back of her workout tank top but couldn't make herself swipe it through the lock—not just yet.

Dodge stopped beside her, looked at the room number placard next to her closed door, and shook his head. "You're in the honeymoon suite?"

"That would explain the size of the bed." And the special lotion and oil sampler basket she'd found on the bedside table.

"My mom is always so subtle. Whatever she says, ignore her."

"What about the universe wanting us to get married?" she asked, the need to prolong their talk and needle him a little overwhelming her better judgment.

He looked up at the ceiling and sucked in a deep breath. "Oh God, she told you."

"Like you said…" Harper giggled at May's antics. "She's very subtle. Don't worry. I told her I wasn't interested."

"Not even a little bit?" He turned and edged closer, putting his hands on the doorframe on either side of her shoulders. He didn't touch her, didn't block her in.

Her skin tingled, making her feel every inch of flesh he wasn't touching. If she wanted to, all she had to do was slide her key card across the lock, and she could escape into the safety of her room. She could get away from the constant tug of attraction pulling her closer to him, the unsettled need that made her clench her thighs, and the way he managed to piss her off and turn her on in alternate breaths. The thing was, she didn't want to, and, judging by his knowing smirk, he knew it. But that was't what made her core pulse. It was the look in his eyes again. Hungry. Determined. Possessive. The air practically sparked around them as desire flooded her body—and he hadn't even touched her yet.

He leaned in, his lips close to her earlobe, but maddeningly far away. "Not even after last night?"

"What's one kiss between enemies?" She couldn't seem to help herself from taunting him, seeing how far she could push him before his control cracked.

His hands slid lower on the door, moving from her shoulder level until they were even with the small of her waist. Still he didn't touch her. "Is that what we are?" The key card slipped from her grasp, falling to the carpet in silent surrender. "It felt like that last night."

"And now?" he asked. He tilted the angle of his head so his lips were just shy of making contact with hers.

Dampness soaked through the center of her yoga pants, and her heart hammered in her chest. "No comment."

"Well…" He pushed his body up against her, flattening her between the solid door and his own thick hardness. "Actions do speak louder than words."

His mouth came down on hers, obliterating any possibility of doing something other than kiss him back just as demanding, just as aggressive, and just as determined to control the situation. If he was looking for someone who sat back and meekly accepted, then he was kissing the wrong girl. Those days were gone for Harper. No one was going to manipulate her into doing their bidding ever again. She was her own woman with her own plans, and right now they all centered around Dodge's hefty bulge pressing against her.

"So fucking hot I almost forgot why you're here. If only…" Dodge's lips brushed across her jaw as his fingers skimmed down the length of her arms until his hands circled her wrists. "But both of us can't be in charge." He whipped her arms upward in one fluid motion, wrapping a single hand around her wrists and pinning them above her head.

She watched him through half-closed lids and pressed her shoulder blades against her room door, rubbing her hot center against his thigh. "That doesn't seem fair."

His eyes darkened with lust, and he repositioned his leg, giving her a better angle to press against him. "You know that life never is."

Bracing herself against the door behind her, she raised up on her tiptoes and undulated against his hard thigh. The stretch Spandex of her yoga pants moved with her as she twisted against him, tempting him and torturing herself with a kind of touch that was good but not quite good enough.

"Fuck me, you're not wearing panties, are you?" The words came out in a pained groan.

Score one for her. "Never with yoga pants."

His gaze dropped to where her hard nipples strained against her cotton tank top. "A bra?"

She shook her head. His nostrils flared with desire, and his lips turned up in a predatory smirk that promised every bad thing she could ever want—and she wanted it all.

"So much for being the proper political princess." He kissed his way down her neck before stopping at the base and nibbling and sucking the tender flesh. "There's more to you than that, isn't there? Something wild trapped inside waiting for the right man to release it."

Harper tried to catch her breath. She may have bitten off a bit more than she could chew when it came to teasing Dodge. He was a master at this game. She adjusted her legs, trying to bring them together, but he kept his strong leg between them, angling it so she couldn't move without her covered clit brushing against him. Then he rocked, slow and easy, against her wetness. She couldn't resist. Her body took over, surrendering to the sensation, and she moaned.

"You don't need a man for what you want right now." He trailed a finger across the scoop neck of her tank top as she rubbed up and down his thigh. "You can do it yourself, and I *want* to see you do it yourself, because what I'm going to give you later on, there's no one else in the world who can do that for you. Not you. Not another man. Just me."

Her arms ached from being held up for so long, her heart pounded against her chest like a jackhammer, and if she could form words she would have yelled for him to yank down her yoga pants and touch her wet folds before she combusted. But she didn't. The sensation building inside her was too intense, too strong for her to do anything but be slavishly devoted to its growth.

"That's it," he whispered against her flushed skin. "Ride my leg right here in the hallway where anyone can see. You want to come so bad you don't even care, do you?"

She didn't. The other people. The rest of the world. None of it mattered right now. She moaned and quickened her pace, the thrumming in her core building in strength.

"Fuck, listening to you is making me so hard." He pinched her nipple through her cotton tank top, rolling the tight bud between his fingers with enough pressure to make her legs quake. "Naughty girl, you like getting off in public." He pressed his thigh more firmly against her clit, rubbing it back and forth as she circled her hips. "The elevator just lit up. Someone's coming. The question is, will you before they get here?"

It was too much. His words. The vibrations making her body pulse. The fact that she was fully dressed in a hotel hallway with her arms pinned above her head while she rode Dodge's thigh already so close to orgasm that her toes had curled.

"You better hurry or someone's gonna get a show." He pulled her nipple taut and gave her earlobe a quick bite. "Now."

She came apart. Her back arched, and her entire body stiffened as jolt after jolt of pleasure zapped through her like she'd grabbed hold of a live wire with both hands. The rest of the world melted away, leaving only them. Eyes closed, she dropped her head to his shoulder and tried to catch her breath. Holy hell, it was going to take a minute to come back to reality from that.

The elevator dinged. Harper's breath caught. *Fuck*. She thought he'd been bullshitting about the elevator, feeding a fantasy she didn't even realize she had.

"Dodge," she squeaked out.

He released her wrists and slid his leg out from between hers. Her arms collapsed to her sides, and it took nearly everything she had to stay perpendicular to the floor instead of sliding down the door, thanks to her jellified legs. She couldn't believe she'd done that. Out here. In the hall. With *him*. Anyone could have seen. Looked like New Harper and Old Harper needed to have a talk, because the last thing she needed was to get involved with a man who handed out marching orders with absolute authority.

"Really, I never. First the reporters and now this," a woman muttered.

Dodge turned his body so he stood between her and her grouchy neighbor and glanced over his shoulder. "Evening, Mrs. Vander."

Taking advantage of his distraction, Harper did the first smart thing since agreeing to share her chocolate chip cookie dough ice cream in exchange for whipped cream. She opened her room door, slipped inside, and shut it firmly behind her. Afraid if she tried to move any farther that her legs would give out, she rested her forehead against the closed door.

His chuckle reverberated through the thick oak door. "I never pegged you for a chicken, Harper."

Heat burned her cheeks. "I'm not a chicken. I'm the queen of Irish good-byes." Slipping away unnoticed from political functions had been one of her greatest talents in her former life.

"Sweet dreams then, my liege."

Harper peeked through the peephole in time to see Dodge retreating down the hall. Sweet dreams? She doubted any of her dreams would be of the sweet variety. Hot and steamy enough to melt her pillow? Yeah, that sounded more like what she'd dream about tonight—if she could even sleep.

• • •

Dodge walked a little more bowlegged than usual down the hall toward his suite. Tonight had gone better than expected with her agreeing to the interview...and, if he was honest, a little worse. He couldn't shake the niggling doubt her soft moans had triggered. Either Harper was an expert at pretending to be the nearly innocent ingénue or she really was. Was it possible his grandfather had suckered her into being his spy or was that just his hard-on talking? It had to be the boner. He was never wrong when it came to business. Never.

Chapter Six

The knock on Harper's door at seven in the morning would have woken her up from a dead sleep. However, since all she'd done all night was toss and turn because of an itch she couldn't scratch, the rapping was only a reminder that she hadn't slept, because Dodge Loving had shaken something loose inside her that she doubted would ever fit perfectly back in its former place.

"Room service," a female voice called out.

Stifling her disappointment that it wasn't Dodge on the other side of her door, Harper hustled across the room and opened the door a crack. "I didn't order room service."

The smell of fresh bacon, scrambled eggs, and orange juice that wafted into her room made her wish she had, though. Who knew sexual frustration could leave someone totally and completely famished?

"Compliments of Mr. Loving."

"For me?"

"Yes ma'am, for you." She turned the cart laden with silver-dome-topped plates away from Harper's room. "Of course, I can return it if you want."

Her stomach protested with a yowl. "No, that's fine." She opened the door.

The attendant wheeled the cart in, stopped near the overstuffed chair by the fireplace, and removed the silver domes covering the plates. "We have bacon from the local Watson Farms, scrambled eggs with a dash of paprika, fresh baked biscuits and..." She lifted the smallest dish cover revealing an ice cream sundae. "A scoop of chocolate chip cookie dough with extra whipped cream and cherries."

Looks like she hadn't been the only one who couldn't stop thinking about last night and the possibilities today held. Excitement prickled her skin, giving her just the shot of adrenaline her sleepy brain needed to be fully awake.

"Thank you," Harper said, barely remembering the manners her proper mother had drilled into her.

"You're welcome." The attendant held out an envelope. "From Mr. Loving." She turned and walked to the door. "Whenever you're finished, call the front desk and we'll remove the tray from your room."

Harper mumbled an okay as she slid her finger under the envelope's seal and then withdrew the single white sheet of paper.

Every time I closed my eyes all I could see was the way you sucked in your bottom lip when you came last night, and all I could hear was your soft moans. This breakfast is my way of bribing you in hopes of seeing and hearing more of you tonight. Until then, I have everything set up for you at eight thirty a.m. in the main library. Thank you for last night and this morning.

He didn't sign the note. He didn't have to; she'd know who'd sent it based on the handwriting alone with its forcefully formed capital letters denoting a dominant, determined personality. So what kind of surprise was waiting in the library at eight thirty? She couldn't wait to find out.

Harper scooped up some whipped cream on her fingertip and sucked it off, wishing Dodge was here so she could see his reaction—the fire and hunger that had blazed front and center last night and wound her up tight enough to...well, get off on his leg. Embarrassment burned her cheeks. *Holy hell.* What had she been thinking? She hadn't—and for someone who'd learned about proper decorum in the cradle, the whole thing was a mess.

Still, she couldn't deny that it did something for her. She grabbed the spoon and scooped up the ice cream. Dessert first might be against the rules for the old Harper, but if she didn't it would melt, and that would be unforgivable. New Harper totally approved. Maybe a no-strings-attached hookup was what she needed. Soon, she'd be back in Washington, D.C., so why not have a little fun while in Wyoming?

One breakfast devoured and a shower later, she glanced at the clock. She had twenty minutes until meeting Dodge in the library. If breakfast was the first surprise of the day, she couldn't wait to see what else he had in store.

Glancing at the mirror, she gave herself a critical appraisal. No amount of cover-up was going to completely disguise Harper's dark circles, and God knew no one had invented the kind of makeup that would hide the extra spark of naughty in her eyes, so it looked like slightly disheveled with a side of lusty giddiness was her look for the day. Not that the shoulder-high stacks of cowboy diaries would notice, but Dodge would. Her heartbeat sped up at the prospect of seeing him again. Desire slid through her veins bringing a little extra pink to her cheeks and making her bra tight as her breasts grew heavy in anticipation. Exhaling a heady breath that sent her bangs flying straight up, she replaced the highlighter brush into its proper spot in her custom-designed travel case and snapped it shut. *Take it down a notch, Harp.*

He's just a guy.

Before her newly found sex-kitten side could remind her of what kind of guy he was, Harper pulled her thoughts away from the brink and hurried over to the walk-in closet. The Michael Kors emerald green halter top jersey dress would do nicely. It was comfortable, casual, and the color made her feel like she could strut the runway. Ten minutes later, she pulled her hair into a low, messy bun and was as ready as she was ever going to be to face Dodge again after last night.

Lucky for her, Mrs. Vander was not lurking in the hallway. She skipped the elevator and took the wide main staircase down to the lobby level. While she was doing her work authenticating May's cowboy diaries in the family's private library upstairs, she'd taken several side trips to the lodge's main library and knew the way by heart. The double doors were closed. She checked her watch. Eight thirty on the dot.

Harper pressed her fist to her stomach, hoping to settle the butterflies swooping around in there, and exhaled a deep breath. Calling up all the image-first lessons she'd learned in how to school her face into a neutral mask, she exhaled a deep breath and turned the doorknob. Dodge sat on the edge of a small table flanked by two men, one of whom held a professional-grade camera. Her step faltered.

Dodge rushed over, his smile doing a number on her and overwhelming the nervous buzzing sounding in her ears.

"Harper." He held her hand, sending jolts of electricity up her arm. "Thank you again for doing this." He turned to face the other men. "Let me introduce you to Brian Haley and Steve Carmichael. Brian here is the editor of the *Freemont Daily*, and Steve is the newspaper's photographer. They'll be doing the interview."

Her stomach dropped to her toes and then dug its way several feet down into The Retreat's foundation. Nausea replaced the butterflies, and the sharp sting of betrayal snapped her spine straight. Like a total idiot, she'd forgotten that Dodge didn't just want her, he wanted something *from* her—for her to sacrifice her privacy and lose her job for the sake of the The Retreat's super-secret guest.

"Nice to meet to you, gentlemen," she said through gritted teeth. "Mr. Loving, may I speak to you outside for a moment?"

"Of course. We'll be a second, guys." The certainty in his gaze wavered, and he leaned in closer to whisper. "Are you okay?"

"I'm fine," she shot back in a low tone. "I prefer not to commit murder in front of witnesses."

• • •

Dodge closed the library door behind him with a quiet *click* that echoed in the deserted hallway. Most of The Retreat's guests were either still asleep or being treated to in-room dining at this hour, which is why he asked Brian and Steve to come now. The fewer people who knew about the reporters' presence the better—for Harper and The Retreat. It made perfect sense, although he should have taken the time to explain his plan to Harper, but he'd wanted to get everything in motion before she changed her mind. He wanted her even though he didn't trust her. The hair on the back of his neck lifted as he watched her pace the narrow width of the hallway looking every bit like she was planning to follow through on her whispered threat.

"What's wrong?" Had she changed her mind? Did she want more prep time? Should he have had coffee waiting?

She spun around on her heel. "Are you serious?" Her decibel level stayed low, but that didn't take away from the venom in her tone.

"No, I'm just kidding," he whisper-yelled right back.

"Yes, I'm serious."

"I never agreed to this." She jerked a pointed finger toward the closed library door. "You couldn't take no for an answer so you set it up anyway, and now you're acting all pissed at me? You're a piece of work."

The world screeched to a jarring halt. Dodge's jaw dropped as he tried—and failed—to make sense of her words. She said she would, just last night. "What the hell, Harper, that's not funny."

"No, it's not." Her pale cheeks had turned a splotchy red, and her brown eyes had become so dark with fury that they were nearly black.

She nailed him to the floor with a look that challenged him in a way most people wouldn't even dare to chance—and for good reason.

"I've spent my life making other people's lives easier, no matter how negatively it affected me. I should have known better last night. I knew you wanted something *from* me more than you ever wanted me. I've been the good daughter and the proper wife and I'm done with that life. I may have stumbled last night, but I'm done with being nothing more than a pawn for powerful men to move around a chessboard."

Fuck. This is what he got for playing along with her game instead of moving forward and doing what needed to be done. "You agreed to this last night in the kitchen. You said 'I will do that'."

"I said 'I will do that' meaning I would *think* about the interview."

"That's not the way I remember things." He squashed the sliver of doubt flickering in the back of his mind and ignored the tickle of conscience. What's done was done. This was the right course of action when dealing with a corporate spy and blackmailer, no matter how they'd gotten here.

Harper threw up her hands with a frustrated groan

before lifting her bangs and flattening them across the crown of her head. "Is there a tattoo visible only to assholes that says 'please fuck with me'? No? I didn't think so." She let her hair drop and shook her head at him. "Do you ever listen to anyone but yourself?"

The question jabbed into him, slicing a path straight to that ember of doubt he hadn't managed to snuff out, which moved him from annoyed confusion to pissed off defensiveness in a heartbeat. "I listened a lot to you last night in words and moans."

She inhaled a sharp breath and flinched back. "You did *not* just go there."

Fuck he had. Regret at how he'd lashed out pinched his lungs together, and he reached out for Harper, something more than the need to beat her at her own game pushing him into action. "I'm sorry, I shouldn't—"

She sidestepped his touch. "That makes two of us. Now if you'll excuse me, I have a job to do that will keep me as far away from you as possible for the next few weeks."

Not even the sight of her perfect ass swaying under her green dress made watching her walk away any better. Sure, he'd crossed the line with the last comment, but that wasn't any reason for going all drama queen. She'd taken the ingénue role a little far. If she was hoping to goad him into following her, then she was about to find out how wrong she was. *Of all the…* Oh, screw it.

If she wouldn't accept his apology for taking her at her word, then he sure as hell wasn't about to chase after her and beg forgiveness. He didn't do that. Never had. Never would. He'd provided the most efficient solution to *both* their problems, and she'd gotten stuck on semantics. He didn't have time for that, not if he was going to figure out exactly what she and his grandfather were up to, keep Garth's location a secret, and make sure The Brasch Group deal went off without a hitch. Priorities. He had his in the right order, and nothing was going to deter him, especially not a devious redhead with a penchant for corporate spying, ice cream, and public sex.

Shoving his frustration into a black hole where most people kept their hearts, Dodge opened the library door with a feasible lie on his lips about Harper's disappearance before he'd even crossed the threshold.

. . .

Dodge's office was the one place in The Retreat that was supposed to be his own. Instead, when he pushed open the thick door, he found his brothers lounging around the oak paneled room like it was theirs. Stone was laid out lengthwise on the small couch with his cowboy hat tipped forward to cover his face if not his snores. Griff sat in the guest chair tapping away on his cell with his feet propped up on Dodge's desk. Dodge slammed the door shut with enough force to rattle the pictures on the wall and wake up Stone.

"Don't you two have somewhere else to be?" He shoved Griff's feet off his desk and circled around to sit in his chair.

"Who peed in your cornflakes?" Griff plopped his boots back up on the desk.

He pinched the bridge of his nose and closed his eyes. "Harper Conner." She of the perfect pink lips, low alto moans, and mile-wide stubborn streak.

Griff's boot heels hit the floor with a loud thunk as he straightened in his seat. "Oh, do tell."

So he did, starting with their discussion over ice cream last night in the kitchen and ending with her unprovoked hissy fit outside of the library this morning—leaving out what had happened in the hall last night. By the time he finished, his youngest brother was grinning like a fool who thought he'd won the lottery, and the middle Loving son had gone back to pretending to sleep on the couch.

"So she thinks that you only hear what you want to hear?" Griff asked, sarcasm as thick as molasses in his voice. "I'm fucking shocked. Aren't you totally surprised, Stone?"

Stone shrugged his shoulders but kept his eyes closed.

"Look." Griff tipped his head toward Stone. "He is so blown away that he's speechless."

As if Stone had ever been called a chatterbox in his whole damn life. Dodge rammed his hand through his hair and flipped on his computer monitor, the screen showing several emails with the subject line: MEDIA INQUIRY.

Fuck me. He did not have the time nor the patience for this shit plus his brothers.

"Don't you have an outing to take guests on today?" Dodge checked his watch and rounded on his other brother. "And aren't you supposed to be giving riding lessons in twenty minutes?"

Neither moved.

"Now if I didn't know any better, I'd think that Harper hit a nerve of our dear big brother's," Griff said as if Dodge hadn't all but ordered them out of his office.

Stone blinked his eyes open and nodded. "Yep. I'd say she took a sledgehammer to it."

They both turned to face him, grinning like a pair of deranged cowboys.

Dodge averted his gaze to his computer screen, focusing with such intensity that if he'd been a comic book hero, lasers would have shot out his eyes. "She didn't hit a nerve, she's just wrong."

"So she *did* agree to giving an interview?" Griff asked, practically rubbing his hands together with glee. "She batted those big brown eyes of hers, leaned forward to give you just a little more than a peek at those great tits of hers, and said

'Yes, Dodge, you hot hunk of man, please violate my privacy and set up an interview that I've made perfectly clear I don't ever want to do.' That's how it happened, right?"

The little nugget of doubt, the one quietly insisting he'd twisted Harper's answer for his own benefit, grew three sizes. Closing his eyes, he pictured her in those skintight yoga pants and tiny little tank top that did nothing but better frame her luscious tits. They'd sat across from each other, then he'd moved to her side and did his little song and dance. She'd said she'd think about it. He asked her if she really would. She said she would do that. Realization poured over him. He heard she would do that and then filled in "do the interview" all on his own. *Fuck.* He'd blown his opportunity to find out more about his grandfather's plans by jumping the gun for the interview. Now he had to figure out how to win her over... again.

"Get out," he snarled at his brothers.

Griff stood. "Come on, Stone, let's give bossy big brother an opportunity to lick his wounds in private."

They shuffled out the door. Dodge may have been alone in his office, but guilt sure was taking up a lot of space in his chair, so he did what he always did in times like this when a business deal was at a tipping point—he researched his opposition.

Chapter Seven

After several days without even a flash of red hair, Dodge had almost convinced himself that Harper had literally locked herself up in the family library surrounded by musty old books. Not that he'd been looking for her. He just kept happening to find himself in the parts of the lodge where she'd be. His steps slowed as he walked down the back hallway leading past the family kitchen.

Light filtered out from underneath the kitchen door—not enough for the overheads to be turned on but just enough to give whoever was inside the ability to walk around without hammering her hip on the stainless steel prep tables on her way to the freezer. Harper? He checked his watch. Not midnight yet, but who else would it be? The kitchen staff had left hours ago, and the rest of the family had tucked into their rooms for the night while he'd been in his office thanking God and the universe for the media's short attention span.

Every last photographer and media truck had departed from The Retreat's front gates this morning after a teen pop star had been busted on the state line with a suitcase full of

Colorado-legal pot. The reporters might be back but, until they were, he had more time to concentrate on other things, like perfect pink lips and soft moans, the nagging feeling that he was missing something in his research. Turns out his grandfather was a big campaign contributor to Harper's dad's campaign war chests. It was a tenuous tie but that, along with her coincidental meeting with his mother that led to her coming to Wyoming and her refusal to do the interview, should have set off his alarm bells. But they didn't.

He'd talked to nearly every staff person at The Retreat and no one reported being questioned by Harper. She hadn't been near his office to take a sneak peak at his files, he knew because his security system was topnotch. Really, she hadn't shown any signs of spying, so she was either really damn good, or he'd made a seriously dumbass assumption.

His hand rested on the brass plate of the kitchen's swinging door. He should go in to double-check to make sure nothing had been left on that shouldn't be—or that there wasn't a stray reporter hiding inside. And if he happened to find a particular redhead licking her ice cream spoon clean, well then she'd have to talk to him instead of avoiding him, which had been her MO for the past few days. And then he'd be able to figure out if she was working undercover for his grandfather.

His pulse picked up as he pushed open the door and walked inside.

"Hey there, Dodge." His mom sat at the little table against the north wall, flipping through a yoga magazine and holding a cup of chamomile tea, judging by the scent.

Dodge's fine-tuned mom-o-meter started dinging like he was the Titanic and she was the iceberg. So far, she'd been pretty low-key about her matchmaking designs, but he'd known it wouldn't last forever. He couldn't backpedal out of here yet or she'd know he'd been looking for Harper.

His step lost a little oomph, but he continued forward.

"You're up late."

"I knew I needed to be if I was going to catch at least one of you in here." She took a sip from her blue cup that read NAMASTE. "She's not here."

"Who?" Keeping his gaze away from his mom, he scanned the kitchen for an excuse. The freezer. Harper wasn't the only one who could get late-night munchies. He could play this off and get out before the world's most icy inquisition could begin.

"Who? Harper, of course." Light and breezy, her voice followed him across the kitchen.

His ass tightened. "Who said I was looking for her?" He yanked open the freezer door. "I was looking for—" He grabbed a pint of ice cream from the freezer and held it out toward her. "This."

"Got a sweet tooth all of a sudden, huh?" May asked, the arch to her eyebrows and tilt of her head screaming out "bullshit."

"It's not all of a sudden." Just since Harper arrived, a fact he just barely managed to keep to himself.

"My mistake." May closed her magazine and shoved it to the side before turning her full attention on him. "I guess it seemed like you'd been doing things a little bit differently since she got here."

He'd been spending a helluva lot of time in the kitchen lately, but otherwise it had been business as usual. "I don't know what you mean."

"Don't lie to your mother, Dodge. It's a fool's errand." May got up and carried her teacup to the sink where she hand-washed it with her signature speed and efficiency.

"Okay then, how have I been different?" he asked.

She twisted the washcloth, squeezing out all of the excess water, shook it loose, and folded it neatly across the bar dividing the double sinks. Nothing unusual in her actions, but it was as if she'd taken almost too much care with each move, drawing it out and losing her signature alacrity. The last time she'd acted so hesitant had been after he'd found his grandfather's letter, right before she'd sat a sixteen-year-old him down and explained why they never heard from or saw her side of the family and why the color of his skin meant he never would. His gut twisted with a sick sense of anticipation. Whatever came next, he wasn't going to like it.

She smoothed her hand across the washcloth one final time and turned to face him, an unusual sadness shadowing her familiar green-eyed gaze. "You've been acting like my father."

"That's not true. I'd never act like him."

"What? Like a man who is beyond determined to force the world to reflect his vision of how things should be even if that means disregarding others' wishes and pleas for privacy? Even if it means thinking the worst of folks on only a thread of information?"

Where his dad had railed loudly and with exuberant hand motions, his mom had always delivered censure clothed in a velvet glove of brokenhearted disappointment. It drained all the bluster and bullshit right out of him.

"Griff has a big mouth," he grumbled.

"True." She laughed. "Look, I know how you feel about your grandfather. I know all about the real reason why you want to take The Retreat global—to show your grandfather all that he lost by cutting off contact with us when I married your father." Her knuckled hand turned white in her tight grip. "But the universe doesn't work that way, Dodge. Everyone has to learn for themselves at their own speed and at the right time. Just like I can't do a thing to persuade you to stop wasting your energy trying to prove a bitter old man wrong, you can't force him to change his thinking, either."

Maybe not, but that wasn't the point. It never had been. "That's awfully Zen of you, Mom."

She smiled, the natural sparkle returning to her eyes, the

same shade as his own, maybe even the same shade as his bastard grandfather. He'd never asked, and he wasn't about to now.

"It's not Zen," May said. "It's what loving your father taught me—to see which battles really mattered and which ones weren't worth the fight. You need to figure that out for yourself before you turn into the one person you hate the most."

That hit too close to home, the truth of it reverberating up his spine. But he wasn't about to turn into his bastard grandfather. He was going to make him pay by taking away the thing he loved more than he did his own daughter.

"I'm going to make the deal with The Brasch Group happen." The declaration came out strained, as if the words were strangling him.

She shrugged her narrow shoulders. "You probably will, but that won't change the universe's plans for you." She held up her left hand and fiddled with the simple gold band on her ring finger.

That was his mom, all right, as subtle as a bull in a china shop. Still, the move back to familiar territory allowed the bitterness he wrapped around his shoulders whenever the topic of his grandfather came up to slide right off him. It lightened his shoulders and allowed him to feel other things like the wet condensation from the pint of ice cream pooling in his palm. *Harper.* In the span of a week she'd become his charmed tormenter or cursed angel of distraction. If his mother wouldn't take this news and run straight to the paper to place an engagement announcement, he would've asked her advice about the chances of Harper being a spy. Figuring out the truth of that had been his real reason for skulking around the kitchen—mostly.

"And the universe told you to put Harper in the honeymoon suite?"

"Oh no. That was motherly interference." She gestured

toward the ice cream with one hand as she removed two spoons from the drawer with the other hand. "You better take that up to her before it melts."

"I told you already, this is for *me*." That didn't stop him from taking both spoons, though.

"Well then." She straightened to her full height and gave him a quick peck on the cheek. "Get your epinephrine pen ready for when you go into anaphylactic shock."

Blinking in confusion, he glanced down and read the label on the carton: pistachio crunch. The little green nut of doom mocked his insistence that the ice cream was his. He opened his mouth, but nothing came out.

His mom shook her head and patted his cheek with her paper-soft palm before leaving him in the middle of the kitchen with a melting pint of ice cream and the certain feeling that his mother and the universe were conspiring against him.

. . .

Harper didn't sulk. She plotted.

Marching from one end of her ginormous suite to the other, she dredged up every Machiavellian scheme to get back at an enemy that she'd learned at her father's knee and—just like she had for the past few days—came up with bubkes.

When it came to teaching Dodge a lesson about bulldozing over everyone else in order to get what he wanted, she just didn't have the heart. It wasn't like it had been with her ex-husband. Dodge hadn't invited the reporters over to save his own skin; he was looking out for his family business and his guest's privacy. If she were in Garth's just-out-of-rehab shoes, she wouldn't want to have to worry about photographers skulking about trying to catch him holding a glass of clear liquid that *could* be vodka. If it wasn't for the threat of losing her only source of income, she would have done the interview the first day he'd asked. When he'd offered to help her find another job…well, that had her thinking. But after how he acted, she had to admit the job finding help was probably another manipulation to get what he wanted.

So since her heart wasn't in finding a get-even-fast plan, she'd retreated to Old Harper's avoidance habits that would do an ostrich proud, and that old familiar hemmed-in feeling that picked at her very last nerve had her twitching and fidgeting like a kid in church.

Sick and tired of being sick and tired, she threw out her arms and fell backward onto the oversized four-poster bed. Sinking down into the fluffy, sinfully soft duvet, she stared up at the sheer white fabric forming a canopy above the bed—it was one more thing in the unabashedly romantic room that made her think of Dodge, and not in the manner in which she should. The fantasies she had of watching his sinewy forearms as he slid his hands up her parted thighs had kept her awake and staring at that damn princess canopy more nights than she cared to remember since he walked into the library a week ago and tried to fire her. The memory of the fantasy alone made her nipples pucker against the worn Book Nerd T-shirt and dampened the cotton center of her sleep shorts.

Ideas big enough for an orgy ran through her mind about what she'd do to that man if he were spread out before her on the bed, as she slid her fingers under the elastic waistband of her shorts. She could lick a path from his hip to the base of his cock, following the *V* line of muscle on his lower abdomen. She'd watched him arrive back at The Retreat after a long run, seen him lift his shirt to wipe the sweat from his face, and gazed in wonder at the lean, muscular lines on display. Sucking hard on her bottom lip, she pushed her fingers through her slick folds to her sensitized clit. The merest touch made her spine bow and started a buzz in her thighs that promised a mind-melting orgasm. How even the idea of touching him did this to her, she had no fucking clue.

Someone knocked on her door and she shot up, heart hammering against her ribs. She yanked her hand from its warm home. "Who is it?" Damn, her breath sounded ragged.

"Ice cream delivery." Dodge's voice came through loud and clear.

Dodge! The man she was pissed at but mentally fucking stood on the other side of her door. Now that wasn't awkward at all.

Drawing a blank on the proper etiquette for this situation, she went with the first response that popped in her head. "What kind of ice cream?"

"Pistachio."

"I don't like that kind." She crossed her fingers behind her back—there was no kind of ice cream she didn't like. Slinking off the bed so he wouldn't hear the mattress springs, if that were even possible, Harper held her breath and prayed he'd accept her answer.

"Are you crazy? It's the best kind. I'm allergic to it, and I still want it."

A swing and a miss. She tiptoed to the door and looked through the peephole. He stood in the hallway holding a small tub of ice cream and wearing a chagrined look on his face. Damn her mutinous body, she responded instantly to both with her mouth watering and her thighs clenching. He needed to go so she could get back to her totally ineffectual plotting instead of eye fucking him through the peephole.

"I've given up ice cream." With her luck, she'd end up lactose intolerant if she kept lying like this.

"That's unfortunate. That means I'll have to eat this, and I get balloon lips whenever I have pistachios." He leaned in close to the door as if he knew she was barely restraining herself from flinging it open. "You will call 911 for me, right?"

"Probably not." The way her body was humming, she'd elbow the paramedics out of the way to give him mouth to mouth herself. God, she was fucking pathetic.

He tapped a quick beat on the ice cream lid. "Then the only other choice is for you to open up and take the ice cream before I eat it. Then we can talk, and I can grovel until you forgive me."

"No, the choice is for you to leave." *That's right, brain, take the lead on this one because the body is leading you astray.*

"If this is the only way to get you to talk to me, then I guess I don't have any other choice." He popped the lid and stuck in the spoon.

Harper froze. It could be his attempt to fake her out—a lame one, but a trick all the same. But if it wasn't and he had some kind of allergic reaction... She slipped the chain free and opened the door halfway, holding it in place with her foot. "Are you *really* allergic?"

"You want a doctor's note?" He gave her a naughty grin that would have melted her panties if she'd been wearing any.

He was not to be trusted. She *knew* this, but as long as she could keep a door between them, there was no reason she couldn't have her ice cream and eat it, too. Now that was a compromise her brain and body could agree on—mostly.

Keeping her gaze locked on the frozen pint, she tried her best to ignore the man holding it as she reached through the narrow opening, swiped it from his grasp, and hip checked the door shut before he could sweet-talk his way inside.

"Hey," he half hollered and half laughed. "We were supposed to talk."

Ice cream in hand, she slid down the door so she sat on the floor with her back against it. "So what's stopping you?"

A thunk sounded low on the door. "A big, hand-carved piece of oak." His voice came through lower. He must have sat down on the ground, too.

"I can hear you through it just fine." She took her first bite of the green ice cream that reminded her a little too much of the color of Dodge's eyes. It was a sweet, but hollow, victory.

"You're a real hard-ass."

"I learned the hard way."

"Tell me about it."

His warm tone snuck through the crack between the door and the wall, warming her from the inside out and tempting her compliance. "Why should I?"

"Because who else can you tell?"

"Who said I wanted to?" *What's private stays private.* Her mother had said it enough times that in another era Harper would have embroidered it on a sampler and hung it on her bedroom wall.

"Everything about you screams it. The only reason you're so tightly wound is because you haven't been able to let any of the ugly just hang out."

What would that be like? Just being herself and not wavering between the proper political princess Old Harper or the tough-as-nails New Harper? The question frightened and excited her. Both were images created out of necessity and the need for control—the first of others controlling her and the second of her holding the reins. That moment of clarity when she'd slapped her ex-husband had been as close to the real her as she'd ever been. If he continued to tug on the thread with his unwavering calm, the covering holding the real Harper in a cozy but too tight cocoon would unravel. Who would she be then?

She ate another spoonful of pistachio ice cream as she rolled the idea around in her head. "How do I know you're not going to run off and tell the world?"

"Because telling guests' secrets would ruin The Retreat's reputation for privacy." No hesitation. No hemming and hawing for some version that would be most palatable. No spin to appease his audience, even if in this case it was just her instead of a gaggle of voters.

"Enough procrastinating." He tapped on the door, the reverberation vibrating up her spine. "Spill your secrets, Harper. What happens in the hallway stays in the hallway."

Heat bloomed in her cheeks at his words. He'd protected her from the overeager eyes of Mrs. Vander when Harper had gotten carried away in the hallway the other night. Now wasn't that a politically correct way of saying "had an orgasm against his leg in public." Chuckling despite herself, Harper shifted to a more comfortable position and scooped up another spoonful of ice cream. "I overturned hundreds of years of family tradition."

"By slapping your husband on TV?"

"No." She shook her head. "By doing what you advised. I didn't seethe only on the inside. I let my ugly hang out for the world to see, and that's just not done."

The level of pistachio ice cream in the pint dropped as she told Dodge about growing up as a potential president's daughter. Boarding school. Debutante school. Elite Ivy League private university. Her parents' schooling that centered on the proper way for a popular politician's daughter to behave at home and in public. None of them had been what anyone with half a heart would call touchy-feely. All of it culminated in her practically arranged marriage to the up-and-coming senator from Vermont.

"Saying it out loud makes it sound all the more bizarre. I was an eighteenth century daughter in a twenty-first century world, and I never thought twice about it. I did what I was told."

"So what made you change?"

On the next breath she was tossed back in time to that moment when her husband, who'd publicly humiliated her by cheating—repeatedly—turned to her at that press conference with every expectation that she'd fall in line with the strategy.

That she'd forgive him so the voters could, too. She should have been furious, but she was too brokenhearted when she realized that she'd never given him or anyone else reason to believe that she wanted to be more than a pawn in someone else's political schemes. Where there should have been fire, there had been only ice.

"I couldn't do it anymore." She inhaled a shaky breath. "Standing on that dais with the press chomping at the bit a few feet away and my ex-husband on his knees in front of me after I told him that the press conference was the last thing I'd ever be doing as his wife, I realized that he didn't believe me. He didn't take me any more seriously than anyone else in the world. Despite my perfect GPA, the functioning brain in my head, and the fact that it wasn't the 1700s, he—along with everyone else—had accepted the perfect political princess image as the real me. I didn't even know who I was anymore. All I knew was how to act as the power behind the throne, doing whatever it took to further the ambitions of those around me. It may not have started with me, but I'd allowed the farce to go on for much longer than it should've, and *that* infuriated me."

The epiphany had hit her with the force of a wrecking ball, shattering every false belief into a million pieces. "With that single slap, I broke free. I'm never going to go back to being the old Harper ever again. I'm my own woman and not a pawn in someone else's plot and plans to be moved around the board as he or she sees fit."

She'd been on a high until the next morning paper hit her door with a thud, followed shortly thereafter by her mother in full-on dowager duchess mode as if by will alone the older woman could turn herself into the ever proper iron-fisted women in the Regency romances Harper loved to read. But she hadn't relented. That had been the first small step toward independence and being in charge of her own destiny.

"So what's next for such a rabble-rouser as yourself?" Dodge asked, bringing her back to the present.

Wasn't that the question she seemed to always be asking herself now? She demolished another bite of ice cream, relishing the sweet, nutty taste of the fast-melting treat.

"Soon, I'll be done cataloging May's cowboy diaries, and I'll go back to Washington to reboot my life." She dropped the spoon into the nearly empty pint, the declaration feeling as hollow as her ice cream victory earlier. "And adding about a million hours of cardio to my to-do list."

"I'm sorry."

"I said cardio," she repeated louder than the first time. "For my giant ass from eating all this ice cream."

"One, your ass is amazing. Two, I'm sorry for acting like a jerk and setting up the press conference. You were right. I only heard what I wanted to hear. I have a bad habit of doing that."

The ice cream pint slipped in her grasp. She may not know Dodge as well as her body thought she did but apologies were about as foreign to his type as ancient Greek. "Who are you, and what did you do with Dodge Loving?"

"Cute."

"I am, but seriously, what gives?" She turned her head so her cheek rested against the door, imagining—however ridiculous it was—that he was doing the same.

He exhaled a heavy sigh. "You said you'd think about talking to reporters and all I heard was 'I will.' Sometimes I get so focused on what I think needs to be done that I lose track of everything else."

She trailed her fingers across the smooth, varnished wood as if she were touching him. "You should stop doing that."

"Hey, I'm working on it. So are we good?"

What had those self-help books she'd downloaded said? That the first step is admitting you made a mistake? That sounded right, and she wanted to believe. If she could change, couldn't he? That was even scarier to contemplate than her own transformation.

"Are you really allergic to pistachios?" *Baby steps, Harper, baby steps.*

He laughed. "Yes."

"Are you going to wait for your brain to catch up to your mouth next time?" She set the ice cream pint down on the floor near the wall.

"I'll try."

It was crazy, but she believed him, right down to her toes. *Must be the ice cream talking—or the universe, if she listened to May Loving.* Whatever it was, it was something, and she needed to get rid of the door between them. Harper scooted over so her back was against the wall instead of the door and reached up to release the latch. "Dodge—"

She turned the knob, and the door flew open with such force it banged against the opposite wall. Dodge, who must have been leaning against it, fell backward, landing on his back.

"Oh my God, I'm so sorry." She scrambled to his side and leaned over him, brushing her hands across his shocked face. "Are you okay?"

He didn't say anything, and Harper filled the silence with imaginary scenarios involving concussions and amnesia. Fingers shaking, she combed them through his short, coarse black hair. Then, he leveled his should-be-patented-as-a-lethal-weapon grin at her and winked one of his green eyes.

"If I say no, will you kiss it and make it better?" he asked.

Relief whooshed through her, and she laid her head on his chest over his fast-beating heart. "You have a one-track mind."

"Oh no, I've already thought up at least five ways this can go." He glided his fingertips across the bare skin of her arms, reminding her all too well of what had happened last time he'd done that.

Desire pooled deep in her belly, warm and heavy. It turned her limbs languid and her breasts heavy with want and need. She straightened her arms and raised herself up from his muscular chest as she swung her leg over his prone position so she straddled him. This time she was the one in charge, and she'd dictate the pace. She undulated her hips, rubbing herself against the hard bulge behind his zipper.

"No." She grasped the hem of her T-shirt and swept it off, then leaned forward so her breasts swung an inch above his hungry mouth. "I only see one way."

Dodge moved beneath her, raising and rotating his right leg enough to kick the door to her room shut. "Great minds, huh?" He lapped at one hard nipple and circled it with his tongue before drawing it into his mouth.

"Something like that." Harper closed her eyes, unable to process any other senses while he touched her, his caress inciting a raw and dangerous yearning that threatened to either drown her or make her levitate right off the damn floor. She'd never wanted anyone the way she craved Dodge Loving. If this was the universe talking, for the next few hours she was going to damn well listen.

"What is it about you?" she asked more to herself than to him.

He released her breast and grabbed her hips, holding on tight as he rolled her over so he was on top. "I was wondering the same thing about you, but I'm not about to question the universe on this one."

The last bit came out muffled, because Dodge was yanking his shirt over his head as he said it, but it didn't matter. At the first sight of his sinewy chest, hard abs, and the deep *V* of muscle by his hips, Harper lost the ability to comprehend any words beyond "faster," "harder," "now," and "fuck me."

Chapter Eight

Dodge had been hard as a fencepost before, but one look at Harper spread out before him on the soft carpet and his balls tightened. After their talk he knew in his gut she wasn't his grandfather's corporate spy, just like he knew that she could never find out he'd started his seduction as a way to get the truth out of her. If she did, she'd be gone before he could get an explanation out. Their time was limited before she flew back to Washington, D.C. and out of his life. He meant to take advantage of every moment.

Her long hair fanned around her delicate face drew his immediate attention, but it was the sight of the stiff peach-colored tips of her full tits that grabbed ahold of him and squeezed the air out of his lungs. They tasted like vanilla, smelled like cocoa butter, and puckered perfectly underneath his tongue. They were magnificent.

Harper cupped the soft flesh, squeezing them. "Stop staring and touch them." She bit her full bottom lip and glanced up at him through thick lashes.

"Is that a request?" He leaned down and blew a soft

breath against her nipples, but didn't touch—not yet. Some pleasures needed to be drawn out and savored.

Her eyes fluttered shut, and she shivered beneath him. "It's an order."

"I don't take orders." He grazed her peach tip with the prickly day's growth of beard on his chin, relishing her quick gasp and quiet moan.

"You only give them out, huh?" There was too much desire in her voice for there to be any room for the snark her words would carry under other circumstances.

"Exactly." He applied the same soft air, hard scruff treatment to her other nipple, the intensity of her wanton response making it harder for him to take it slow, to push her right on to the edge of need where nothing existed but pleasure.

She planted her feet on the floor on either side of his hips and lifted herself so that her center fit perfectly against his rock-hard bulge. "Do you always get what you want?"

"Yes." Temptation—she was the word personified.

Undulating against him, her lips curled with come hither promise. "Good."

He leaned back on his heels and hooked his fingers into the waistband of her sorry excuse for shorts, inching them down over her round hips. "Stand up."

Without hesitation she lowered her luscious ass to the carpet and raised her long legs straight up in the air. "No."

The challenge made his cock jerk with anticipation, and he dragged the tiny shorts off her legs in one quick motion, throwing them across the room. "Stand up." He barely recognized his own voice, it was so strained with hunger for this woman who'd driven him to the point where he stalked The Retreat's kitchen at midnight in hopes of running into her. "Please."

This time she did.

Still kneeling before her, Dodge grasped her hips and spun her around so her perfect ass was at the same level as his face. Round and high with a small tattoo of an infinity symbol made out of books inked into her skin where her lower back met her butt, it was a sight to behold. His mouth went dry. He didn't know whether to kiss it, smack it, or dive right in. Instead, he went with squeezing the soft globes as he traced her tattoo with his tongue.

Harper's head fell back, her long tresses falling across the smooth expanse of her back. He gathered up the strands in his left fist, pulling them to the side as he kissed his way up her spine until he stood behind her, one hand holding her hair taut and the other curved around her hip, pulling her tight against him. She was so soft and supple where he was hard and yearning. He didn't have to sink his fingers between her legs to know she was wet and ready for him. He knew it as surely as he knew that he'd be lost the moment he sank himself deep within her folds. So he'd draw it out for both of them, dance on that edge as long as possible, until they couldn't hold out any longer.

"Spread your legs for me." He sucked her earlobe into his mouth, grazing the tender flesh with his teeth. Instead she ground her ass against him, making his balls tighten.

He clamped his jaw tight and buried the urge to bend over and take her right now. He couldn't. Not yet. They needed to get closer to that edge, and he knew how to do it. "You wouldn't want me to open those curtains, would you?"

She gasped and tried to turn her head to look at the floor-to-ceiling windows lining the opposite wall covered by dark blue curtains, but he held her tight. She trembled, and her breathing came in quick bursts as her brown eyes darkened with hunger. The other night she may not have realized how turned on making out in public would get her, but when she came fully clothed just by rubbing herself against his thigh, she found out what her kink was, and so did he.

"Your room faces the country, but with the lights blazing in here you wouldn't be able to hide yourself from anyone who happened to walk by." He glided his right hand around her hip, spreading his fingers wide so they covered her flat belly. "They'd stop and watch as I sank my fingers deep inside you, cupped your tits, and pinched those big nipples of yours. Out there in the darkness, hidden from your view, they'd get to see everything." He pressed against her lower abdomen with just enough pressure to make her whimper with want for more. "How you suck in your bottom lip when the orgasm builds." He slid his fingers lower, parting her tight curls. "How you can't stop from responding to my touch and answering back with moves of your own." He nipped at that sensitive spot where her neck met her shoulder. "How you come against my fingers and how you lick them clean afterward." He stopped right on the edge of her cleft so close to her swollen clit that she mewled in frustration. "Now." He tapped against her sensitive skin. "Spread your legs." Without a sound, she did.

For a moment, all he could do was be grateful that she'd taken mercy on him before he lost control completely and forgot about taking things slow. She wasn't the only one affected by the little fantasy he'd spun. "Thank you." He slid his fingers home. "So soft and slick for me."

"Yes." She rested the back of her head against his shoulder, eyes closed and lips parted.

It gave him the perfect top down view of Harper. It humbled him. "You are the most beautiful person I've ever seen. I could watch you like this, flush and wanting, forever."

"I hope not. I plan on coming tonight." She rubbed her ass against him, her heat seeping through the material of his pants.

"Don't worry, you will." He increased the pressure of his touch as he circled her clit, relishing her responsiveness as her thighs began to tremble and she bit down on her lip—all signs of a building orgasm. "But not yet." Withdrawing his fingers as he released her hair, Dodge drew in a deep breath in an effort to calm the lust raging through him.

Harper took a step forward and spun around. "Are you teasing me, Dodge Loving?"

The front view of her abundant curves made his balls ache for release. "Only for a little while."

"Well then..." She glided her nails down his abs as she lowered herself to her knees before him. "You won't mind the same treatment."

His brain short-circuited as soon as she undid his belt. When she popped his pants button, his vision narrowed until all he could see was her. His heart rate increased with every millimeter she lowered his zipper. As soon as her fingers wrapped around his hardness, pulled him from the confines of his boxers and bent to lick the moisture on its tip, he realized he was in trouble, but it was too late to stop now—even if he'd wanted her to.

She tilted her chin so she looked up at him, her big brown eyes full of just the kind of wickedness he needed more of in his life. "Look at the size of that."

"Stop, you'll make me blush." Damn, he had too many clothes on. He stepped out of her grasp and made fast work of flipping off his shoes and shucking off his pants and boxers.

"No." She shook her head and crawled close enough that her lips nearly brushed his cock. "I'm going to make you hotter than that before I'm done."

Fuck if he didn't believe her.

She started with her hand, slow and steady, before licking her lips and taking him inside her hot mouth. There wasn't any rushing. It was divine torture to watch over and over again as his cock disappeared into her mouth and bumped against the back of her throat. She brought her free hand up to her tits and pulled her nipples as her mouth engulfed him. He didn't move. He couldn't. For the first time in his life, he loosened his grip on the control he valued above all else. Then she hummed and flicked her tongue against his hardness as she raised and lowered her head, and he lost track of anything other than her and how she seemed to know what he wanted, needed, without ever being told.

His balls drew up as he approached the point of no return. The buildup for both of them hadn't started tonight. Everything had begun the moment he'd walked into that library intent on firing her. "Harper." Her name tore from his throat in warning.

In response, she wrapped her fingers around the base of his cock and squeezed—firm and assured—before letting his dick slide from her mouth. The movement stopped the building orgasm in its tracks as effectively as he'd ever done himself.

"That's…" He blinked in surprise.

She arched an eyebrow and released him. "What, you don't think you're the only one in the world who plays the edge and release game, are you?"

"I'm done playing."

"Thank God." She glanced down at his pants crumpled on the floor. "Condom?"

"No." Now wasn't that the universe grabbing him by the balls and twisting.

Her eyes went wide. "You don't have one in your wallet?"

"Do I look like a frat boy?" He could call down to the front desk; that wouldn't be awkward at all tomorrow morning. He could find Griff. His brother would never let him forget the emergency, but it would be worth it. He grabbed his pants from the floor. "I'll be right back."

"Oh no, you're not leaving this room." She tugged his pants from his grasp, curled her fingers around him, and began to wreak havoc on his hard cock. "Looks like we'll have to find another way to spend our time."

It was tempting, so very tempting, but he needed to bury himself inside her more than he needed to get off quick. "It'll just take me a minute…"

Harper dropped to her knees and took his cock deep into her warm, wet mouth, and he lost the ability to form words. She used just the right amount of suction that added to the tease of her tongue sliding up and down his dick's sensitive underside. In his position, there was no way he could fool himself into thinking he was in charge anymore and—for once—he didn't give a damn.

He dragged his gaze upward from the sight of her smeared lipstick-covered mouth sliding along his hardness to her red hair spilling around her creamy white shoulders and on up to her brown eyes that had turned black with lust. God she was beautiful…feisty…smart…and talented beyond belief with her tongue. Dodge hated her ex-husband for hurting her almost as much as he despised whomever she'd be with after she left Wyoming. She went down on him in one long motion, swallowing him to the base and stripping every pretense away. The urge to claim her as his own rushed to the forefront…but he didn't have the right. Harper wasn't his no matter what the universe had supposedly declared.

She let out a muffled squawk around his cock before releasing him and rocking back onto her heels.

"Are you okay?" he asked, wondering what in the hell he'd done wrong.

"Better than okay." She got up and hurried over to the unlit fireplace and the large basket sitting on the hearth. "I unwrapped this the day I arrived thinking it was a fruit basket like a normal hotel would leave to welcome a new guest—then I found this." She yanked a bullet vibrator still in its original packaging from the basket. "There has got to be a condom in this basket."

• • •

Harper set the cherry flavored massage oil on the hearth. She tossed the two-ounce bottle of warming liquid over one shoulder. It landed on the plush fur rug with a sound. Next, she pulled out a pair of pink, fuzzy handcuffs. *Now those could be fun.* They went on the hearth next to the massage oil. There was no way a basket like this wouldn't include condoms, probably glow in the dark ones. She pushed her hand down to the bottom of the basket and fished through the contents until she felt a familiar four-cornered object.

"Aha!" She yanked her hand out of the basket, lifting the small foil rectangle in triumph, and then pivoted on her knees so she faced Dodge. "You said this *is* the honeymoon suite. I'm guessing that's why there's a condom, edible oils, and a sex toy basket to welcome me."

She would have giggled at the horrified look on his face if it hadn't been for the fact that he stood naked in front of her in all of his too-damn-hot-for-reality sexiness.

He shook his head. "That's not normal hotel protocol, no."

Her mind went blank for a second and then the obvious answer filled the void. "So your mom—"

"Let's leave her and the universe out of it." He strode over and swiped the condom from her grasp as he wrapped an arm around her waist and pulled her tight against him. "We have more important things to do."

Anticipation sizzled in the fraction of an inch of air between them. Everything was set; all they needed was that final spark to set it ablaze.

Her stomach fluttered. Tonight was probably a mistake, but damn, what a glorious mistake to make. After a lifetime of doing everything by the book she needed this break, this fantasy. With less than two weeks to go until she had to leave Wyoming, why not burn up the sheets with Dodge?

She tilted her chin so she could see his green eyes that sparkled so bright against the setting of his dark skin—the combination as breathtaking as he was. "Then what's stopping you?"

His answer was a kiss, the kind of toe-curling, mind-erasing, set-your-body-on-fire kiss that made the rest of the world disappear, because it no longer mattered. At least for tonight Dodge was hers, and she meant to make the most of it.

Wrapping her arms around him, she returned the kiss meeting his tongue thrust for thrust. His hands were everywhere, stroking, kneading, pushing her further down the path to ecstasy. It was almost more than her body could take. Desire soaked her inner thighs, and her nipples ached with the need to be touched, pinched, tasted. His fingers slid down her stomach and farther south until he buried them inside her wet folds and began to stroke her. It was good, amazingly good, but her core clenched with the need for more.

"Dodge," she whimpered.

He didn't speak; he didn't need to. In the next heartbeat, he'd wrapped his strong arms around her and lowered her so she was on her back in the middle of that white fur rug, its softness the perfect balance to Dodge's hardness. She splayed her legs wide, needing him inside her.

He tore the condom wrapper open with his teeth, rolled it on, and positioned himself at her damp entrance. "Look at me."

She did. She couldn't have said no to anything right now; the lust flooding her body had drowned out any little voice of doubt. Need and hunger shone from his face, and not just for anyone, but for her. The realization shook something loose

within her. In all her life no one had ever looked at her quite
like that.

"So beautiful." He entered her in one slow but sure
stroke. "So damn beautiful."

He paused, letting her adjust to his size, before
withdrawing and starting the process again. She wrapped her
legs tightly around his waist, tipping her hips to deepen the
angle so the head of his cock rubbed in just the right spot
with each thrust. In and out, forward and back, the opposite
forces working together to take them both to the edge and
push them right over.

It started in her calves—the tingling that built with each
breath, each thrust, each undulation against him. She was
close, so damn close. She just needed…"Faster."

"Whatever you want, honey." He tightened his grasp on
her hips, lifting her higher and increasing his pace while at
the same time moving his thumb so he caressed her swollen
clit.

The touch was all it took, and pleasure crashed against
her as her orgasm hit with the force of a tidal wave. Her entire
body bowed as she cried out in mindless ecstasy, blocking
everything except her connection to Dodge and the sound
of his strangled cry, and he thrust one final time deep within
her.

He collapsed next to her, one arm slung across her
middle. It took a minute for the last waves of pleasure to
abate and her to become aware of her surroundings. With
the lazy satisfaction of a cat who'd eaten all the cream, she let
her gaze travel up Dodge's sinewy body. The divot by his hip
she planned on tasting later. The hard outline of his abs that
she wanted to trace with her tongue. His thick biceps and the
curve of his broad shoulders that she… The wicker basket on
the hearth caught her eye.

"I've never been so glad to get a gift basket in my life."

She sighed.

"I'll say." Dodge scooped her up in his arms and strode toward the honeymoon suite's canopy bed.

She giggled. "Remind me to write a thank you note to your mom."

He grumbled some response about crazy women and the universe and tossed her into the middle of the gigantic bed before sliding in beside her and dropping the comforter across them both. She rolled onto her side to face him, her breath finally returning to normal, and cuddled into the crook of his arm. Under the influence of his deep breathing, her eyes fluttered shut. Tomorrow she'd decide if this had been the best mistake or another in a long line of regular mistakes, but until then, she'd give in to the hope that this time everything would work out, and that her time in Wyoming would include a welcome diversion in the form of a brawny and brainy corporate cowboy who loved to get his way and get her off.

Chapter Nine

Barely conscious and with last night's lusty dream still real enough that her thighs were sore, Harper rolled over and snuggled deeper into the feather pillow. Five more minutes. Her alarm would go off soon anyway. She always set it fifteen minutes before she really needed to get up to account for her inevitable snooze-a-thon. Double-checking that the alarm was ready to go was always the last thing she did before—

She jackknifed up in bed, panic waking her more effectively than the loudest alarm. Sunlight streamed in through the wall of windows, a pair of spotted sandpipers perched on her balcony railing. The pillow next to hers was empty, but the still-warm sheets proved that her dream had very much been a reality. But where was Dodge?

Gone.

She pulled the comforter over her head, blocking out the sunlight but not the reality of her situation. Embarrassment burned her cheeks, and a quaky sensation jumbled her empty stomach. She'd had a one-night stand, and he'd disappeared without even a whispered good-bye. *New Harper needed to learn impulse control.* Adding it to her mental to-do list, along with the hours of cardio to burn off all the ice cream, she tossed off the comforter and got out of bed.

Nine days and she'd be back in her tiny little Washington, D.C. apartment, rebuilding her life one day at a time. Until then, she'd concentrate on work—and only work—cataloging and authenticating May's cowboy diaries. At the pace she was going, she'd be able to finish before the deadline and get away from The Retreat and all of its temptations of the human and ice cream variety.

The door lock turned with a mechanical buzz. Harper gasped, grabbed the comforter, and wrapped it around her nakedness before picking up the alarm clock on the bedside table and raising it above her head so she could bean her intruder. The door opened, pushed by a room service cart covered with silver-dome-covered dishes that jiggled and clanked as it moved forward. Dodge grinned at her as he maneuvered the cart into the room with one hand and, with the other, pointed to the Bluetooth in his ear.

She dropped her arm, and the alarm clock's corner jabbed into her thigh. Yelping with surprise more than pain, she flopped down onto the bed and tried to make sense of the situation. He'd come back. Pressing a fist to her stomach, she tried to squash the fluttering hope inside, but it was too late. A two-week fling without any possibility for a future might be the thing to help her transition to the new, improved her.

"Yes, I understand your position completely. We at The Retreat share Brasch's commitment to our guests, high standards and, above-all, discretion." The door swung closed behind Dodge. "The reporters have left the premises and caused barely a blip of concern for our guests."

Leaving the cart in the middle of the room, Dodge walked over to her with a determined strut that knocked the sense right out of her head. Stopping at the edge of the bed, he hmmed and um-hmmed the person on the other end of the line as he tugged one corner of the comforter free. He traced a finger across the curve of her now-exposed shoulder, following the line down her arm. Anticipation skittered across her skin, and impulse control became the least of her worries. Releasing the comforter's other corner, she sat up straighter and basked in the heat from his hot gaze on her bare breasts with their puckered nipples.

His nostrils flared. "I'm sorry, Jean-Luc, can you repeat that?"

She caught sight of the fast growing bulge pushing against his inseam and couldn't look away. Licking her lips, a naughty idea began to shimmer in the back of her mind, one that the new Harper loved. Scooting to the mattress's edge, she traced his cock's outline with her fingernail and was rewarded when it twitched under that barest hint of a touch. Well, she wasn't the only one in favor of her idea.

"Exactly," Dodge said to his mystery caller, watching her every move.

Keeping her gaze on him, she slid her palm up his leg to his waistband. It took seconds to unsnap his top button and lower his zipper, but she inched his pants and boxers down to his midthigh with deliberate slowness. The vein in his temple pulsed, but he didn't make any move to stop her as he continued to make noncommittal noises to the caller.

A lick, a taste, more than a little tease, and she'd leave him in peace to finish his call, but the man offered more temptation than she could say no to. At least that had been the plan, but as soon as she touched her lips to him she couldn't deny herself, especially not when she heard his sharp intake of breath and felt him push himself against the seam of her lips. Opening her mouth, she took him in, flattening her tongue and undulating it against him as she drew him in deeper.

For as unhurried as she'd been last night, she cranked up the pace now—sucking, licking, and stroking him at a speed guaranteed to push him as far as he could go, take him out of his comfort zone. He'd tormented her last night to a state of near mindless bliss; time to return the favor. She cupped his balls, and they tightened in her hand. Understanding his body's cue, she increased her speed.

"Jean-Luc." His voice cracked on the other man's name, and he raised an arm above his head, gripping the bed's solid wood post tightly. "When we partner our brands on this new enterprise you can be assured of our commitment to being an exclusive and secure haven for high-profile guests who value their privacy above all else." His jaw clenched and he squeezed his eyes shut as he came with a nearly silent groan. "No, I'm fine… *Au revoir*, Jean-Luc."

He slapped his hand against his ear, presumably ending the call before sighing and opening his green eyes. "You are some kind of trouble."

Harper winked up at him and shot him a sassy grin. "Who knew?"

She couldn't believe she'd done that. Before Dodge she was a lights off, missionary position kind of gal. Now? She'd given him a blow job while he was on the phone. That was wild, and she couldn't wait to see what kind of trouble she could get into with him next.

• • •

Two hours, one cold breakfast, and three orgasms later, Harper was thousands of feet in the air above the Grand Tetons on a helicopter tour with Dodge.

When she'd taken the job at The Retreat her mental image of Wyoming was a black void. It was a blank space that she'd flown over a million times in her family's private jet on the way from one coast to the other. The beauty spread out as far as she could see, took her breath away—tall mountains with snow-covered peaks even in the summer, crystal blue lakes, and a river that wound through it all. Gorgeous didn't begin to cover it.

"Pretty, isn't it?" Dodge asked over the low-frequency static buzzing on the headphones he'd given her before takeoff so they could chat during the noisy ride.

"What is it?" Heat flushed her cheeks. *That didn't sound dumb at all.* "I mean, I know they're mountains but..."

"It's the Grand Tetons." He chuckled. "The mountain range goes on for forty miles, but the park is eighteen million acres. "

"That's huge." She'd never seen anything like it. You could fit four hundred Washington, D.C.s in that space, which would make the whole finding a parking spot a ton easier.

"Grand Teton needs its space." He pointed out the window at a huge mountain in the distance. "You want the story?"

She nodded and pressed her cheek to the window for a better look at the Wyoming scenery. The great outdoors had never been her thing, but seeing it from the sky on a personalized tour from the man who'd rocked her world last night and this morning...well, the new her wasn't the type to turn down that experience.

"French trappers named the range the three teats, but we Anglicized the name—and niced it up—so it became The Grand Tetons," Dodge said. "That's the highest peak at more than seven thousand feet. See the river?" He pointed to the winding waterway. "That's Snake River which feeds Jackson Lake and several other small lakes. Plus, there are dozens of small glaciers hidden in the mountains. The park has some of the oldest rocks in the U.S. Park System."

"How old?"

"Only two point seven million years." He nodded his chin toward the windshield. "That is an almost perfectly pristine ecosystem, and you can find plants and animals that have been around since prehistoric times. Also, the best trout in the whole wide world."

Harper pivoted in her seat to get a better look at Dodge. In jeans and a T-shirt wearing aviator sunglasses and even with the dorky headphones, he looked as comfortable and sexy in the helicopter's pilot seat as he did in a tailor-made suit while sitting behind his desk at The Retreat. She'd been shocked when he'd told her he was flying them on this surprise tour, but she shouldn't have been. The man wasn't ever *not* in charge, even when he was off work. The realization should have sent her running for the mountains in the distance instead of ditching work so she could spend more time with Dodge.

"I can't believe you talked me into this." The words came out before she could stop them.

He unleashed his panty-dampening grin. "I'm a great pilot."

Shaking her head, Harper giggled. Who'd have ever thought Mr. Business-Always-Comes-First would turn out to be such a flirt? "I don't even take sick days."

"Me either, but maybe it's time we both let loose a little."

The growly edge to his voice, the same one he'd had when he'd had her naked in front of the window last night, made her breath catch. Warm desire made her breasts heavy, and she crossed her leg in an effort to ease the need tightening her core. "I don't know if my body could take it if I was any looser."

"Now that sounds like my kind of challenge."

"Smartass." They banked around a mountain, and a huge crystal blue lake lay spread out before them. "What is that?"

"Jackson Lake. It's fifteen miles long and one of the

largest high altitude lakes in the country."

"Are we going swimming?" Not that she'd brought a suit, but skinny-dipping sounded like another first to enjoy with Dodge. Just the idea of seeing his muscular frame dotted with water made her nipples peak.

"Not unless you want to freeze your ass off. The water never gets above sixty degrees." He laughed and eased the helicopter down. "That's where we're going." He pointed to a small island in the middle of the lake. "Sandpiper Island."

"Is this where you take all your morning-after dates?"

"Only you."

A giddy, fizzy feeling made her lungs lighter and took away her ability to make a saucy remark, so she covered the lapse as best she could by taking in the scene. Tall pine trees covered half the island, while a rock beach and flat grassy area dominated the other half. A large white tent was set up on the edge of the tree line, its sides billowing in the wind created by the helicopter. The whole glamour meets nature scene looked like something out of a fashion magazine.

"Looks like someone's having an event." The lucky soul.

Dodge nodded. "That someone is us."

Her stomach took a nosedive that had nothing to do with the drop in altitude and everything to do with the man in the pilot's seat. She blinked away her surprise, thankful for her sunglasses' dark lenses, and pressed her lips together to still the trembling. He'd planned the whole thing for her, not because he needed something from her, but because he wanted to. Even as a child her birthday parties had been carefully orchestrated events that doubled as networking opportunities to further her father's career or raise funds for her mother's favorite charities. Gritting her teeth, she inhaled a calming breath and eased back from the emotional ledge.

The helicopter landed with a soft thud on the grass. Dodge flipped some switches, killed the engine, and opened his door. "Don't get out yet." He hustled around the front, ducking down to avoid whacking his head on the blades, and opened her door. "Watch your head." He pointed up at the blades.

Harper got out, her hair lifted by the breeze coming in off the lake. "Thanks."

Hand-in-hand, they walked across the clearing to the tent. Large pillows covered the floor and surrounded a small table covered in fresh wild flowers and food that smelled like heavenly sin. A small silver cooler sat on the ground next to the table. Dodge flipped the lid open with the toe of his boot. A pint of chocolate cherry fudge ice cream, a bottle of whipped cream, and a jar of cherries were nestled inside.

Bracing herself with a palm against his broad shoulders, she raised herself up on her tiptoes, relishing the heat of his body against hers, the musky male scent of his skin, and the solid reassurance of his strong body. Being so near to him was like catnip—she just couldn't get enough, and the contact high was too good for her to listen to the doubts Old Harper whispered in her ear. There'd be time for that later. For the next few days, she would play things by the heart.

"A girl could get used to skipping out on work to hang out with you." She brushed her lips across his, but the brief contact wasn't enough, and she deepened the kiss. It was more than thank you, more than I want you… It was the first step in a journey leading to her new life.

Pulling back while she still could, Harper paused. Barely hearing the island's namesake birds above the sound of blood rushing in her ears, she couldn't look away from Dodge. *Dial it down, girl. It's just a fling.* In less than a week she'd be back home in Washington, and there wasn't space in her new life for a corporate cowboy in Wyoming.

Dodge exhaled a deep breath, and the genial tour guide look returned. "Now that's exactly the kind of reaction I was hoping for." He reached inside the cooler and retrieved the ice cream. "What do you say to having dessert first?"

. . .

Dodge sank back into the pillows next to Harper and closed his eyes, inhaling the strawberry scent of her hair. Over lunch they'd talked about everything and nothing. He couldn't remember the last time he'd lingered over a meal with a date instead of rushing to get naked. They weren't exactly taking it in the normal order, but even he couldn't argue with the rightness of how it had turned out. It wasn't permanent, but he didn't have time or space in his life for that—he didn't think he ever would. After the Brasch deal closed in a few days, his life would be all about taking The Retreat global. His revenge on his grandfather would lose its luster if he only won in the short-term. Of course Harper would be on her way back to Washington soon, so what was the harm in a little fun? As long as she never knew about his initial intentions, everything would be fine.

He cracked his eyelids, sneaking a look at her. She sat with her arms wrapped around her knees and watched the pelicans swoop down and scoop fish up out of Jackson Lake. The sunlight caught in her hair, giving the red strands a blond hue. Without stopping to think, he reached out and wrapped a silky strand around his finger. Harper turned her head and brushed a kiss across his finger, the brief touch as potent as if she'd reenacted the blow job from this morning. And to think he'd tried to fire her, catch her in the act of being a corporate spy, and think she'd actually follow through on her threat to tell the press Garth was at The Retreat. Damn, he was a real idiot sometimes.

She returned her attention to the lake and the mountains on the other shore. "It's just beautiful out here, it's like nothing could ever knock it down."

"There are hundreds of small earthquakes each year in the Tetons as the ground shifts." He encircled her waist and pulled her back so she was tucked against him, her curves fitting against him like she'd been made for him. "But the changes are so small that no one notices, at least not until there's a big one."

She turned so her cheek rested against the pocket of his shoulder and snuggled in. "A series of little earthquakes, now that could describe my life up until now."

If she called being publicly humiliated by her jerk of an ex-husband and stalked by paparazzi because her family was practically on the Kennedy-Clinton-Bush level of politically famous small earthquakes, he couldn't imagine what she'd describe as a big one. "Are you reforming yourself?"

"I am." The slight vibrato in her voice gave away her nervousness but didn't take away from the strong determined bass deepening her tone. "My new life starts as soon as I get back to Washington. This job was my first step toward total independence."

He did a double take. "You've never had a job before?"

"No." She laughed. "Not unless you count being a stereotypical political princess daughter and wife."

He tilted her chin up so she had to look at him. "I don't think there's anything typical about you." And he meant it. She was unlike anyone he'd ever met before—equal parts intriguing, alluring, and mystifying. Puzzles were his specialty, and he'd yet to crack the code that was Harper.

"You say the prettiest things." She brushed a kiss across his lips. "I suppose you started working on the day you were born."

"Not quite." There were family pictures of a swaddled baby version of him in a bassinet while his mom taught yoga to The Retreat's guests, but they'd waited for him to get a business degree before really letting him get his fingers deep into the business. "The joy and agony of a thriving family business is that it's always there, and you can never get away from it."

"Do you want to leave?" she asked. "Is that what the call this morning was about?"

He stiffened, the festering anger at his grandfather turning his blood to ice. "No. That was taking care of old business."

Harper propped her chin up on her hand and cocked her head. "Sounds like there's a story there."

If it had been anyone else asking—even his family—he would have blown off the question. But with Harper the truth always seemed to leak out of him.

"My grandfather owns a chain of luxury hotels across the Northeast. That's how my parents met. My dad went to Boston to apply for a job. He got it and then he met my mom at a company meet and greet. They fell in love, and a few months later I was more than just a gleam in my old man's eye. When they told my grandfather she was pregnant and that they were going to get married, he told them that he'd disown my mom before allowing her to marry a black man. That went over about as well as you would expect."

"I'm so sorry." Sympathy shining in her eyes, she leaned down and kissed his cheek.

"It's his loss." He shrugged as if the rejection of his parents…of his brothers…of himself didn't matter when in reality it had burned a hole right through him. "And he's going to see that for himself in a few days."

"What happens then?"

It hadn't been easy to find out what his grandfather's plans had been, but Dodge wasn't one to give in because the road was tough. "That's when The Brasch Group is going to officially choose The Retreat over my grandfather's company as its partner to develop an exclusive line of international luxury resorts."

She laid her head back on his shoulder, and a loud silence descended before she sighed and shook her head. "So it's just revenge."

"No, it's good business." And it was, but that wasn't all it was. "But you're right, taking something away from the man who mercilessly cut his own daughter out of his life because of who she fell in love with? That sweetens the pot." The old man's empire was in trouble, according to Dodge's sources. Losing this deal could mean disaster for his grandfather's hotels because they needed the influx of cash The Brasch Group was bringing to the table. When he didn't get it, then the old man would understand rejection where it mattered the most—his bank account. "Once The Brasch Group's representatives arrive and see for themselves that no one can beat The Retreat when it comes to discreet, high-end hotels, we'll sign the paperwork, and everything will be right in the world."

"So you're starting a big earthquake."

Certainty filled him. "Don't you know it."

Chapter Ten

Nearly a week of spending as much time as possible with Dodge after their romantic picnic, lingering over finished work had become the name of Harper's game. The mile-high stacks of cowboy diaries were gone from her desk and stored once again on the custom-built shelves lining the private library on The Retreat's top floor. Her evaluations were complete, and dollar values had been assigned to each diary in May Loving's unique collection. The only thing standing between her and the end of this job was the simple and quick task of finalizing the certificates of authenticity—well, that and the man standing in the library's open door. Keeping her head down, she peeked up at him through her lashes.

Dodge rested one shoulder against the doorframe, a one-sided curl to his lips, as he watched her. He'd been there for nearly ten minutes. Not talking. Not coming in. Not going out. Just watching, seeing how long it would take before she'd push away her paperwork and beg him to come in and lock the door behind him. It hadn't happened enough to be a routine but, over the past six days, the library had seen enough action to make her life feel like it would fit right in with the Wild West shenanigans the cowboys had written about in their diaries. Their nights spent in her suite were for taking their time, but the afternoons in the library? Those were for hot, fast fun.

Still, instead of calling him in, she kept doodling on the legal pad in front of her, taking time out to suck on the tip of her pen or drag it across the *V* neck of her blouse as she contemplated the gibberish she'd written. Each of Dodge's barely perceptible sharp inhales in reaction only emboldened her. She'd leaned forward, angling her body so her breasts were on display because her shirt just happened to be unbuttoned enough to show off not only the high, round curves of her cleavage but the delicate lace of her bra.

The teasing got to her as much as it did him, making her nipples pucker and setting off all sorts of delicious shocks in her core. She trailed the pen, damp from sucking on it, down her sensitized flesh and into the deep valley between her breasts. The move opened up her blouse even more to his view, and he rewarded her exhibitionist audacity with the firm *thud* of the door closing and the *click* of the lock.

He was across the room before she knew it, standing beside her desk but still not touching. "You're a tease."

She rolled back her chair and swiveled it around so she faced him. "Little ole me?" She batted her eyelashes at him as she widened her legs, the move pushing up her short skirt.

Lust darkened his moss green eyes to the color of the pine trees on Sandpiper Island. "You're not wearing panties."

"Oops." She tugged her bottom lip between her teeth and glided her fingers up the inside of one bare thigh.

He loosened his belt and slipped his top button free. "I have a conference call with The Brasch Group in half an hour."

Looking anywhere besides his busy fingers wasn't

possible, and the dampness between her legs increased as his zipper descended. "That doesn't give us much time."

"Someone shouldn't have spent so much time pretending not to see me." He toyed with his waistband but didn't push them down.

"Who's teasing now?" she asked, her own need turning her voice husky.

Desire rushed through her, warming every inch of her already flushed skin. He knew all the right buttons to push and some she didn't even know she had until she met him— like the decadent thrill she got when she put herself on display for him. Forcing her gaze up to his face, she watched him—as she always did—while unbuttoning her blouse completely.

The air sparked around them, a dangerous combination of sexual electricity and something more potent. Whatever it was, it only happened with him, and she didn't want to be without it, not until she had to be and maybe not even then. Pushing the idea into a dark corner, she gave Dodge a saucy wink as she undid the last button.

"You..." He grabbed her hand and pulled her up from the chair so her body fit perfectly against his. "...are killing me."

"But only the little death." She wriggled out of her skirt— accidentally on purpose rubbing against him as she did so— and then laid back on the desk, letting her bare legs dangle over the edge.

Teasing time was over; after all, it had been their foreplay. Now she was more than ready for the real fun to begin. Dodge moved between her legs and pushed his pants down far enough that his hard cock sprung free. He rolled on a condom and brought himself in her with one firm thrust. It wasn't slow and it wasn't tender, but she loved it, needed it, just like this, because whatever was going on between them wasn't always soft and gentle. It was big and intense and it eclipsed everything else in the world when she was with him.

Their hands were everywhere on each other, touching, caressing, urging each other on, and she gave as much as she took from him. With each in and out stroke, she rose higher, the sensation tightening inside her, blocking out everything else but them until her body couldn't take the pleasure anymore, and her climax exploded.

"Dodge." She muffled her cry into his shoulder as she came, and he buried himself deep within her as an orgasm shook his body.

"Damn, Harper." His low gravel tone battled with the awe in his voice. "You undo me."

She looked up into his green eyes, and what she was about to say died on her lips as her chest tightened. Dodge was not hers. She wasn't his. This was a fling, a rebound, but it was starting to feel like more, and that was a complication she didn't need.

"You okay?" he asked.

Blinking away a sudden onslaught of emotion, she swallowed the feelings bubbling up inside her and said the first non-I-like-you-more-than-I-should thought that came into her head. "Someone needs to take your mind off closing the big deal."

He chuckled. "Are you about to drop an important lesson?"

"Nah, only remind you that there's more to life than rubbing your success in your grandfather's face."

He kissed her neck. "Noted."

An easy lightness lifted her even as her limbs were too heavy to move, and she relaxed back against her desk. Still riding the last waves of bliss, her gaze caught Dodge's and she sighed, content and happy and satisfied beyond imagining. That's when it hit her as hard as a backhand to the cheek. The procrastination. The delays. The slow forward progress.

It was all because she wasn't ready to walk away from Dodge, and she wasn't sure she ever would be.

• • •

Any postcoital afterglow Dodge still had after the world's fastest shower went dark as soon as he stepped into his office and found Frank, The Retreat's head of security, pacing in front of his desk.

"We've got a problem." Frank rammed his hand through what was left of his gray hair, the perma-grimace he always wore etched deeply into his craggy forehead.

Circling around his desk, Dodge asked even though he already knew the answer.

"The reporters are like fucking cockroaches," Frank grumbled, his New York accent as thick as the day he'd started ten years ago. "I get rid of one and two more show up next time I turn on the lights."

Dodge shook out two Tums from the bottle in his top drawer and tossed them back, crunching them to bits with more force than was necessary. Harper wanted him to remember there was more to life than The Brasch Group deal. If she only knew...

The reporters had started showing up again three days ago. Harper's ex-husband's mistress had given an exclusive interview to some trashy tabloid and told the world that the senator from Vermont liked to wear adult diapers during their sordid encounters and had called Harper his mommy and the mistress his babysitter.

It had taken considerable effort to keep the news from Harper, but there were advantages to being in the middle of Wyoming where cell phone service was spotty. He'd ordered the staff not to mention it to Harper and to turn off any televised reports as soon as they'd started. So far it had worked, but the reporters kept showing up.

"What are we up to?" Dodge sank down into his seat, frustration, guilt, and indecision burning a hole through his gut.

"I've tossed that slimy little paparazzi photographer three times for trespassing. No arrests as you'd requested to keep everything on the down low. The more legitimate reporters hang around the gate waiting for a shot. I shooed them off again this morning. The Brasch guys are going to be here in two days to sign the paperwork. They aren't going to like having to drive through a small pack of reporters to get to the front door. You've gotta do something."

He was fucked no matter what option he picked. If he ignored the reporters, the deal would fall through and The Brasch Group would go with his grandfather's hotels. If he sent Harper to the wolves, she'd never forgive him. He'd crossed her once on that topic and wasn't going to do it again. Where was a celebrity with a drug habit when he needed one? In hiding right here at The Retreat, which, if they knew, would make the reporters at the gate turn rabid in order to get an exclusive on the recently dried-out Garth Hampton's whereabouts. Dodge's gut cramped. He was between the Grand Teton mountain and a hard place.

"So what's the plan, boss?"

"The nuclear option." He grabbed the phone and dialed. There was a chance his plan would backfire, that the reporters could make a national stink and claim intimidation, but to save Harper from having to know the jackals were hanging around—let alone talk to them—he'd risk it. "Sheriff Vista, Dodge Loving here. I need your help getting the press away from here for a few days."

• • •

Sweeping up her messy desk hair—was that even a thing?—
Harper gathered it into a high bun before using her towel to
wipe the fresh steam from her bathroom mirror and checked
her reflection. The shower had frizzed her hair, hence the
bun, but the pink in her cheeks had more to do with Dodge
than the hot water. Once she finally made it downstairs to the
yoga studio for class someone was going to tease her about
wearing makeup.

She signed in on the attendance registry and grabbed
a pair of yoga pants and a tank top and got dressed. She
couldn't delay it much longer; her job was done and she
needed to go home. *Home.* In the past week, Wyoming had
begun to feel a lot more like home than Washington ever had.
She couldn't stay, but that didn't mean she wanted to leave.
More specifically, she didn't want to leave Dodge.

The idea of getting on that plane in a few days made her
sick to her stomach. She'd come to Wyoming for work, to
create a new self-identity, not to fall in… Nope. She shook
her head. She wasn't going to even think that word. The ink
on her divorce papers was still wet. Dodge was her rebound
guy. That was all. That's all it could be.

Two women on one of the afternoon news shows chatted
on the TV screen in her room. Since she'd come to Wyoming,
she'd taken a vacation from political news, but she needed to
catch up. As soon as her plane landed at National, it would
be politics all the time once again; it was the currency of the
nation's capital.

"And we'll be right back after these commercials to talk
about the latest scandal rocking Washington," one of the
hosts said. "It's a real doozy."

The screen cut from the woman in a red power suit to a
commercial for prescription anxiety medication.

"Poor fool," Harper said to herself as she shut off the
TV. There was always some poor sap in the news for idiocy—

their own or someone else's—and was now having the worst week ever. *Been there. Done that.* Didn't wish it on her worst enemy.

She grabbed her yoga mat and a towel before heading out the door and hustling to the yoga studio. May was already there, walking between the mats, making sure everyone had a yoga block and bottle of water.

"Harper." May waved her over. "I saved you a spot here between Amelia Perkins and Skyler Fane. Ladies, this is Harper Conner. Amelia is The Retreat's accounting genius and Skyler is a local kindergarten teacher. It's the first time for both of them, and I thought you might be able to help them out."

"I'm not exactly awesome at this." Which was true. She still had trouble with tree pose.

"Don't be silly. You do just fine." May looked past Harper's right shoulder, and her eyes widened. "Oh, Ms. Finty is trying to do the crow pose without warming up. She's going to fall on her face and break her nose again." She rushed off.

Harper smiled at Amelia, petite enough to make Harper feel like an Amazon, and Skyler, with her friendly, open face, looked like you'd expect a kindergarten teacher to look. "Hi."

"It's good to finally meet you. May has been hounding me to walk away from my desk and into class for weeks," Amelia said as she spread out her mat. "I'm so sorry about the reporters."

"Nice to meet you, too." Harper shrugged and settled into corpse pose. "And at least the reporters are gone now."

"Oh no," Skyler said. "There're several outside the gate and Stone told me they've caught a creepy photographer skulking around the grounds this week."

"What?" Harper sat up fast enough that she got lightheaded.

"You didn't know?" Amelia asked.

Harper shook her head, unease making her skin prickle.

"Um…your ex-husband." Skyler turned a shade of red so bright that until now Harper didn't think could be found in nature. "His…uh…"

"Skank," Amelia said. "The lying bastard's skank gave an interview and said he had a thing for wearing diapers."

"And calling you mommy." Skyler kept her attention focused on the boxed Zen garden at the front of the studio.

Harper went numb. She couldn't feel her fingers, her toes, or the yoga mat underneath her ass. She could still see everything, but it was like she'd lost connection to her body, and her brain was wrapped in a six-foot thick layer of cotton. Her ex had never called her anything but Harper. He'd been a Brooks-Brothers-suit-and-white-boxer-shorts-wearing preppy without a hint of anything beyond every Tuesday and Thursday night vanilla, lights-off-only sex followed by a mandatory shower for them both. Diapers? Mommy? The press would want to talk to her. Ask rude questions. Even as much as she hated it, she couldn't blame them. This was the kind of juicy sex scandal that sold papers and got killer ratings.

"Okay everyone, let's begin." May strolled to the front of the class. "We'll start with sun salutations."

Unable to fight her way through the haze, she switched to autopilot—a skill she'd perfected the summer she was twelve and had to accompany her parents on campaign stops in the sweaty humidity despite having her right arm in a cast that itched like the devil. Sitting in the cool air conditioning with her arm propped up wasn't an option. The Conner family had an image to maintain, and a perfect daughter was part of it. She'd already messed up the picture enough with the cast she'd let her friends sign in messy unmatched markers.

Harper's body moved of its own accord through the class.

Arms up. Back arched. Legs lifted. Warrior pose. Child's pose. Then she was back in corpse pose, lying flat on her mat with her palms facing upward and her eyes closed.

"When you walk back into the world outside these doors in a few minutes, I want you to take with you a little bit of the peace I hope you found here today," May said, her voice calm and quiet. "Remember to breathe deeply, and think beyond the mundane. Do not think of life as something that you must control. Think beyond. Life is not about ceding or gaining control. It is about letting others in and sharing our experiences. Namaste."

"Namaste," Harper said along with the rest of the class as she blinked and came back to herself.

"I'm so sorry," Skyler said as she rolled up her mat with quick efficiency. "I didn't realize…"

"Me too." Amelia wiped the sweat from her brow, still in corpse pose. "I tend to speak first and think second. There's a reason why I spend my day with numbers."

Sitting up slowly, Harper looked at the other two women—one sweaty and spent and the other looking like she could outrun a pack of five year olds, which Skyler probably did on a regular basis. She knew all about snide backhanded compliments and sly critiques. Amelia and Skyler didn't seem the type.

"No big deal." She stretched and sat up. "After all that's happened you'd think I'd be used to these kinds of surprises."

"Well then, in the spirit of sharing experiences, as May said, how about we take you on a girls' night out tomorrow to make up for being a pair of clods?" Skyler asked.

"Promise I'm much more fun when I don't feel like a wet noodle," Amelia said, holding up a two-fingered salute like a Boy Scout.

A light bulb went off in Harper's head. *Letting others in and sharing experiences.* The reporters weren't going to leave her alone until she'd addressed the latest news. The story was too juicy and her family too prominent for them to let it go. That meant Dodge's deal with The Brasch Group would fall through at the first sight of a telephoto lens in the bushes. But if she talked to them, it would cost Harper her job. In all likelihood it would take years to find another position as perfect for her as this one. Was it worth it for a man she'd probably never see again after her plane took off in a few days? The ache in her heart though answered that question in the most succinct way possible.

"What do you say? You coming?" Skyler asked.

"Let's do it," Harper said, a plan that had nothing to do with girls' night forming in her mind. "I gotta go. Just call my room to let me know what time and where to meet you."

Waving good-bye to Amelia and Skyler, Harper rushed out of the yoga studio. She needed to get the number for the local paper and reschedule the interview she'd walked out on last week.

Chapter Eleven

The next morning, Harper patted her hair that was pulled back into a topknot, tucked a stray lock behind her ear, and watched the antique grandfather clock's second hand move another notch forward.

Brian and Steve from *The Freemont Daily* were ten minutes late. A small mound of shredded paper sat in a yellow mountain on her desk, sacrificed to the gods of nervous energy. She sucked in a deep breath and ripped off a fresh sheet of paper. Her plan was more than a little nuts, but even as nervous as she was, she knew it was the right one.

Really, it was a win-win. She'd talk to the local paper and deliver the message she wanted to get out. Once the story broke in the morning, the tabloid reporters outside would lose interest because an exclusive, first-get interview—the kind that came with big freelancer payoffs—was no longer on the table. Once again, Harper would be old news, and the media would be gone from The Retreat's gates before the big muckety-mucks arrived to sign the hotel expansion deal, making Dodge's life so much better.

It couldn't go wrong. She wouldn't let it.

The grandfather clock ticked off another minute, and her phone rang, the quiet sound as loud as a starter pistol in the silent room. *Relax, you dork.* Harper picked up the phone. "Hello?"

"Ms. Conner, this is Paul Esposito at the front gate. I've got two fellas from *The Freemont Daily* down here who swear up, down, and sideways that you invited them on the premises for an interview."

"Great." She did her best to ignore the fluttery feeling in her stomach and put on her game face. "Please let them know I'm waiting for them in the upstairs library."

"I'm afraid I can't let them in, ma'am. Mr. Loving's orders."

Her hand froze mid-stroke in the act of sweeping the pile of torn paper from her desk and into the trashcan. "What are you talking about?"

"No reporters or photographers are allowed in. We've even got a mess of deputies helping to patrol the grounds and keep 'em all away."

"But I *invited* Brian and Steve." She shoved the paper into the trash, her brain rolling through the possibilities to save the interview. Leaving the grounds wasn't an option. The reporters at the gate would see her. She had to get them inside.

"Sorry, ma'am. I just can't—"

"Do you really think I'd do this without Dodge's agreement?" Her cheeks burned. It wasn't a lie exactly, but it wasn't the truth, either. She squashed her conscience into a bite-sized morsel and reminded herself this was for the greater good—hers and Dodge's. Anyway, her father had used this kind of deflection in a million campaign town hall meetings with angry voters, and it always worked.

"I don't have any knowledge of that, ma'am."

Harper pasted on her best political princess smile. The guard might not see it, but he'd hear it in her tone. "Brian and Steve are local."

"I know, they're in my Tuesday night bowling league."

Score. "I can't imagine they're the type of folks we're trying to keep out. Dodge's orders were likely for the out-of-town reporters, the ones stirring up all the trouble. I can't believe Steve and Brian are on some sort of blacklist."

Right up to the edge of that truth cliff without tumbling over into the lie valley. Sure, she was holding on by her toenails, but still...

"It does stretch the imagination," the guard said.

"Exactly," she said. "So I tell you what. Just to make sure there aren't any problems, you escort Brian and Steve to the front door, and I'll meet you there. They won't leave my sight even for a minute."

"I'm not sure Mr. Loving—"

"Don't you worry about Dodge," she said before the guard could wander any further down that path of thinking. "I'll make sure he knows everything, including how diligent you were in your duties. I'll see you at the front door." Now, time to end things on a we're-all-part-of-the-same-team note. "Thank you so much for going the extra mile on this."

"Not a problem, ma'am. I'm just doing my job."

She could practically see the guard's aw-shucks blush over the phone. "And you do it well. See you in a few minutes."

Ten minutes later and she was behind her desk again, but this time, instead of staring at an ever-growing pile of yellow confetti, she was smiling at Steve and Brian as if they were the only people in the world she'd ever wanted to talk to. It was all in the eye contact and the slight curl of her lips—too much non-verbal interest and she looked like a deranged potential stalker, but just enough and everyone walked away happy. She'd gotten the look down doing personal profile interviews as a teenager, but had really perfected it as a senator's wife sitting in on constituent teas and fundraisers. The key was to pretend you were on a blind date with the most interesting person in the world and no one else was there—that and a firm handshake.

"Gentlemen, thank you so much for coming this morning. I apologize again for the delay at the gate."

"Dodge has things tighter than a tick on a bison today." Steve flipped open his notepad. "He must have someone big coming to stay."

Deflect! "Ouch. You know how to prick a girl's ego." She chuckled as the editor turned a brilliant shade of cherry.

"I'm sorry. I didn't mean to imply…"

"I'm just teasing, Steve." She winked at him. "Now I know as editor and chief reporter for *The Freemont Daily* you must be a busy man. So let's get right to it, shall we?"

Steve nodded his bald head and uncapped his pen. "Why are you in Freemont, specifically at The Retreat?"

"I'm here at May Loving's request to authenticate some very interesting diaries she's collected over the years." She waved her hand at the leather-bound cowboy diaries on the closest shelf. Some were worn and had been thumbed through by hundreds of unknown hands. Others were practically as pristine as when the cowboy or cowgirl first cracked the spine. What each diarist had in common, though, was the absolute commitment to living the life they'd chosen for themselves.

"So you're not here hiding out?" Steve asked.

You couldn't get much farther from Washington D.C. than Wyoming, which is why May Loving's job offer had been so appealing, not that she'd admit that for public consumption. "You saw the reporters gathered at the front gate. If I was, I'm not doing a good job of it."

"Fair enough." He scratched a few notes on his narrow notepad. "What do you think of the latest revelations about your ex-husband?"

She curled her hands into fists, grateful the desk between her and the men kept them from picking up on her tell. "Truthfully, I try not to think about my ex-husband at all."

"So no comment on the whole mommy thing?" Steve kept his observant focus steady on her.

Straightening in her chair, she met his gaze head on. "I think mothers are fabulous, but my ex-husband never thought of me as his."

Twenty more minutes of parry and evade questions, interrupted occasionally by the photographer's flash, and Steve flipped his notepad shut.

"Anything else I should have asked that I didn't?" He tilted his head to the left. "Anything you wish people knew about you?"

That stopped her. She was nearly thirty years old and she was just getting to know herself after letting everyone else in her life define her. What should people know? That she was done being a pawn in someone else's game, a salve for someone else's wound, or the goat when someone else lost. She was just Harper Conner, woman remade, but that, of course, was not the kind of answer she needed to give Steve.

"I think people know too much about me as it is," she said. "I grew up in the spotlight. There are only so many political dynasties left in this country, and I was born into one of the largest. I understand the fascination, even if I don't share it. However, I've chosen a different path for myself than the one that had been chosen for me. We all should be allowed to choose our own path in life, and mine takes me out of the spotlight for good."

The men said their thank-yous as they got up. Harper circled around the desk and walked to the door. Interview completed, the stroll to where the guard was waiting to take Steve and Brian to the gate was filled with polite conversation about the weather. The summer sun warmed Harper's skin as soon as she stepped out onto the wraparound porch.

The photographer came to an abrupt halt in front of her, and she nearly plowed right into him. "Forget something?" she asked.

Brian turned, his gaze flicking from one end of the porch to the other, lingering on the western side where the guests tied up their horses before a staff member walked them out to the barn for a rubdown. "Can I get a couple of shots here? The lighting is great."

Harper looked around. No one else was there, but the idea of a guest spotting the photo shoot didn't sit well with her. The last thing she wanted was to help Dodge by causing more problems. "You didn't get enough during the interview?"

"Just a few more." He shuffled to her left and held the camera to his eye. "Five quick shots before the light changes."

Another quick glance; the porch was deserted except for Paul, the guard, who was typing away on his smart phone. No guests to get mad about a photographer taking some pictures. "Okay. Go for it."

Five clicks later and the three men piled into Paul's golf cart and headed back to the front gate. The story would go out on the web tonight and in tomorrow's paper, Steve had assured her. By the time The Brasch Group representatives arrived in the afternoon, the media would have gone off to find other targets, and Dodge wouldn't have to worry about sleazy tabloid photographers popping up out of the bushes to ruin his plans. She couldn't wait to tell him the good news.

. . .

Less than twenty-four hours before closing the biggest deal of his life, and all Dodge cared about at eight that night was getting through The Retreat's lobby without getting stopped by a guest with a problem or a staff member with a question so he could get to Harper's room. The deadline clock on The Brasch Group deal wasn't the only one ticking down.

He hit the main staircase without a second look from anyone in the lobby. Most of the guests were packed inside the wine bar where the large television was tuned in to some entertainment gossip show. For once the human obsession about knowing everything about everyone else was working in his favor and he double-timed it up the steps.

In a few days Harper would be gone, too, a fact that had wormed its way into his subconscious and kept popping to the forefront at inopportune times—such as this morning when he'd started to think of ways to get her to stay longer. Who would want to miss watching the July fourth fireworks from Sandpiper Island? Or the county rodeo in August? Or the leaves starting to turn in September? The truth was he didn't want to miss her at any of it.

Pausing outside of the honeymoon suite, Dodge's heart rate was double what it should be for jogging up the stairs and hustling down the hallway. He should be in his office, going over the numbers one last time to ensure everything was perfect for the final presentation. He should be meeting with The Retreat's department heads to answer any questions, assure them that their jobs were safe, and explain the possibilities once the deal came through. He should be conducting a personal inspection of the hotel making sure everything was in its proper place. But he wasn't. He was outside Harper's door because, on a night as important as this one, he didn't want to be anywhere else, which meant nothing but trouble. He couldn't lose sight of the finish line now, not when he was so close.

Still, he knocked.

The door swung open, revealing Harper wearing the second-skin yoga pants guaranteed to turn his mouth dry and his brain to mush. "I have a surprise for you."

His phone buzzed in his pocket, but he ignored it. "What's that?" He walked in and shut the door behind him.

"I've solved all of your pesky reporter problems." She handed him her tablet.

Distracted by the large photo of her perched on the edge of a desk in the library with her red hair pulled back and looking every bit like the sexiest book nerd of all time, it took him a second to realize what he was looking at. *The Freemont Daily's* website. The headline read: FROM POLITICAL PRINCESS TO CHAMPION OF COWBOY LORE. His phone vibrated against his thigh.

"But your job?" He couldn't believe she'd done this for him.

She shrugged.

"Why didn't you tell me first?" he asked. After everything he'd done, the favors he'd called in to make sure she wouldn't be hounded by the press, she'd flung open The Retreat's doors and invited them in.

"I invited the editor and photographer you'd introduced me to back over for an exclusive interview. It went just like you said it would." She took the tablet from his grasp and kissed him, slow and sweet. "Now without the money for a first-ever exclusive dangling in front of them like a million dollar carrot, the other reporters and photographers will go look for their next big money target. It's only on the web now, but Steve said he'd put it out on the wires so any paper that wanted it could run the story."

His phone went off again. Three times in five minutes meant disaster-movie-sized problems. He pictured the people gathered around the TV downstairs, the photographer on the premises without any prep work to hide their most publicity-adverse guest, and The Brasch Group representatives getting on the plane on their way here now. Dread, ice cold and heavy as a two-ton truck, sank to the bottom of his stomach.

The text message confirmed the worst.

Griff: Deadline Entertainment has pics of Garth Hampton at The Retreat holding what looks like a vodka bottle. It's gone viral.

He scrolled down to the embedded photo. It was grainy, but there was no mistaking the rock star just out of rehab or the redhead on the right side of the frame. Frustration twisted him up inside. So close. He'd been so fucking close to ripping The Brasch Group's investment right out of his grandfather's hands. He'd failed. He'd had the opportunity to right an old wrong, and he'd fucking failed.

He gaze moved to the voicemail icon that showed two messages, both from The Brasch Group's headquarters. Privacy. Discretion. Luxury. Right now The Retreat was batting one for three, and that wasn't good enough to make this deal happen. He was fucked because he'd gotten distracted by a woman he'd known was trouble before he'd even set eyes on her. Forget getting her to stay. She needed to get the hell out of here before she tried to help again.

He pictured his grandfather sitting in his Boston office, scrolling the headlines and seeing the news. Dodge pinched the bridge of his nose and tried to think of a way out of this mess.

"What's wrong?" Harper pressed her palm to his chest right above his heart.

The touch was the perfect reminder of all that could become fucked up when he forgot his priorities. He showed her the text. "Everything." All his hard work, the planning, the confidence that his grandfather would finally hurt for what he'd done, ruined.

Harper took his phone. She made it a few sentences before she raised her hand to her mouth. "Oh no, you have to believe me, I never meant for this to happen."

He wanted to. He really did, but just the sight of her had him rearranging his priorities so that at the top of the list was hearing the sweet sound of her moaning his name. He fisted his hands so he wouldn't give in to the urge to reach out to her. He couldn't lose focus again. That's what had got him in this mess. The woman made thinking rationally an impossibility. If she hadn't ever shown up, The Brasch Group's representatives would be sitting in front of him ready to sign the expansion agreement that would guarantee his grandfather's hotels' failure. Instead, Dodge would be cleaning up her mess.

Harper's hands shook as she handed his phone to him.

He spoke before she could make a sound. "You need to leave."

She flinched.

The move tore at him, but he couldn't give in. She was leaving anyway, had never had any plans to stay. A hard, merciless break was for the best, especially after this fiasco.

A flash of pain reflected in her eyes. "I know you're upset. I know there've been unintended consequences of my interview. Just hear me out, I—"

He had to be ruthless. It was the only way to win—and he always won. "You need to leave The Retreat."

Her gaze fell to the floor, and she blinked several times before raising her face back up to look him in the eye. Her bottom lip trembled, shaking his resolve, but he held tight.

"I was trying to help." She said it so quietly he barely heard.

They were on the edge. Teetering. If he reached out to her now, everything could be different. The temptation to do so finally spurred him into self-preservation mode. He let the emotion drain from his face until there was nothing left but ironclad neutrality.

"A great job you did with that. Now instead of a handful

of snoops, I have a horde of reporters camped out in their news vans outside the gate." Each word out of his mouth was like a jagged knife into his chest, but it couldn't be helped. He couldn't lose sight of his main objective. Not again. "I'll have to *beg* Jean-Luc and the other Brasch Group representatives not to call off their visit after this. Beg. I never beg, but they're ready to sign the agreement with my grandfather's hotels so I don't have another choice. Your help is the last thing I need."

She straightened and raised her chin another half inch into the air. Gone was the woman who'd sighed in awe at her first sight of Sandpiper Island...the woman who'd giggled as she scooped up another spoonful of ice cream...the woman who'd called his name when she'd come in his arms. The woman before him was an ice-cold princess, too far above him to be touched. Her realm may have been political instead of geographic, but that didn't take away from the royal disdain in her brown eyes as she stared him down.

Her lips curled in a contemptuous excuse of a smile. "It wasn't that long ago that my help was all you wanted."

No, that hadn't been all he'd wanted, still wanted, from her—and that was the problem.

"I won't be making that mistake ever again." Dodge swiped his phone from Harper's fingers and strode to the door. He couldn't leave yet, not without knowing for sure. "Just tell me you didn't plan this, that it wasn't deliberate. I'd convinced myself you weren't a spy. Tell me I'm not wrong."

Harper gasped. "A spy?"

"My grandfather owns the company you work for." Saying the words left a bone-deep ache in him, a throbbing reminder of his stupidity in letting himself get distracted and worse... letting himself care. "When you first got here I thought..."

"You thought I was here to sabotage the deal and that's..." Her normally pale face turned ghostly before being replaced with an angry red. "Is that why you...why we..."

Staring at Harper as her chin quivered, he couldn't say anything. What could he say to the truth?

"It doesn't matter." She raised her chin. "For your information, I'm not a spy, but it sounds to me like you are indeed your grandfather's true heir."

"That's low." Anger wiped away everything, leaving only a bitter taste in his mouth.

She brushed the back of her hand across her cheek. "Just get out."

He shut the door behind him hard enough that the crack of wood on wood bounced down the hallway. She was as wrong about him as his grandfather had been to turn his back on his family all those years ago. This is why he didn't do attachments. Spy or not, Harper had been nothing more than a temptation he'd fallen prey to—no more, no less.

Eyes cast low, Dodge barely saw anything around him as he headed down to his office, where he should have been in the first place.

Chapter Twelve

Secluded in his office with the lights turned low to mitigate the tension headache trying to crack his skull, Dodge yanked open his top drawer and grabbed the nearly empty ibuprofen bottle. "Yes, Jean-Luc, I share your distaste of the coverage."

He pinched the receiver between his shoulder and ear so he could use both hands to fight the battle of the childproof cap. At least he had a chance to win that one, not that he was giving up on the other.

"This may not be the time for our meeting," Jean-Luc said. "Perhaps in a few years…"

He shot back the gel caps and swallowed, determination to win over Jean-Luc superseding his need for water. "This is the perfect time for our meeting. You're already in Wyoming. It would be a horrible missed opportunity to go back to France without seeing The Retreat for yourself."

All he had to do was get Jean-Luc on the premises. Once he was here, he'd see for himself all that The Retreat could bring to the endeavor.

The Frenchman sighed. "The reporters are still there for

that rock star?"

"They are." Even though Garth Hampton had all but disappeared. The rock star wasn't answering his phone or his door—not that Dodge could blame him. "But this gives you the chance to see firsthand how we manage in a time of crisis." Every obstacle was an opportunity, and if it wasn't he'd make it one. Harper had been right about one thing—he always got his way.

"I'm not sure it is a good time." The other man said one thing, but doubt lingered in his tone.

Now was the time to pounce. "Jean-Luc, you know almost as much about The Retreat as I do. You know this is not how we normally do business. Come see for yourself that the media is not having an effect on the guests or the daily hotel operations. It may not be as quiet as things are normally, but what fun is it if there is no challenge in life?"

The Frenchman chuckled. "You are persistent."

In that half second Dodge knew he'd won. He relaxed in his chair and let his head rest against its high back. "And you are only a half hour away. Come for lunch."

"*Oui*. Lunch it is, but no promises," he said. "I'll make the stop at The Retreat but only as a courtesy. Your grandfather made a very impressive showing in Boston, and we're ready to ink a deal with him."

The old familiar resentment bubbled up inside him, threatening to drown the elation he'd felt only moments before. It hardened his tone and his commitment to making this visit a success. "Thank you for even that. *Au revoir*, Jean-Luc."

Dodge hung up the phone with deliberate care, his emotions running too close to the surface for comfort. He should be elated, but all he felt was empty. Jean-Luc was throwing him a bone. The deal had imploded when the first report about Garth hit the internet. It would take a miracle to change Jean-Luc's mind. That wasn't the worst, though. The worst was that he couldn't shake the image of Harper trying not to cry as he'd left her room.

· · ·

Four hours. That's all the time Harper needed to finish up her final report on May Loving's cowboy diaries, print out a copy for May, and email a digital version to her bosses back in Washington. Rescheduling her flight home to tomorrow took two phone calls and one ginormous—and very worthwhile—charge to her credit card. Now she had less than twenty hours to count down until her plane took off and she could put Wyoming forever in her rearview mirror, or at least the jet's review mirror, if it even had one. She'd Google it to find out, but the idea of picking up her phone only reminded her of the voicemails and texts from her mother admonishing her for going public with family matters.

She sacrificed her job and her privacy for Dodge, and it had all been for nothing. Everything between them had been a facade. A game of is-she-or-is-she-not-a-corporate-spy that she hadn't known she'd been playing. Old Harper may have been a timid mouse, but New Harper was an idiot.

Scathing reminders of her place in society from her mother and a broken heart—that's what she got for trying to become the new Harper. Who in the hell had she been fooling? No one but herself. She'd come to Wyoming and fallen right into the familiar rut with a man who only cared about using her for his own means and tossing her aside when she was no longer useful. But she had done something new this time. She'd fallen in love with the bastard and hadn't even realized it until he cut her out of his life with the clinical detachment of a surgeon.

"Love is for idiots with high pain tolerance," she mumbled

to herself as she sniffled.

Harper paced from one end of the large honeymoon suite to the other, studiously avoiding even a passing glance at the bed. The room phone rang, throwing off her stride. Dodge? Damn she hated the hope that rose to the surface. "Hello?" There, that sounded almost totally and completely normal.

"Hey, Harper! It's Skyler. Everything okay?"

All right, maybe not perfectly normal. "Fine, just packing up my things." She glanced at the empty suitcases lined up in front of her closet.

"No way, I thought you were here for another week or so."

So had she. "Changed my mind and rescheduled my flight." Her chest tightened, and she bit the inside of her cheek to help herself keep it together.

"Dodge?" Skyler asked.

Enough of a knowing sympathetic ribbon ran through Skyler's one-word question to make Harper figure it wasn't the first time she'd asked it. If anything, the concern pricked her pride even more. "What makes you say that?"

"It's a close-knit community. If everybody isn't up in your business that just means you're dead—and even then there's no guarantee." Skyler paused long enough to suck in a quick breath. "So there's even more reason for our girls' night tonight since we won't get another chance."

Harper caught a glance of herself in the mirror. Scraggly hair. Smudged eyeliner. No lipstick. "I don't know."

"Come on. Who better to hang out with on your last night in town than the two women who know—and will tell you over a pitcher of cheap beer—every embarrassing thing that has ever happened to Dodge Loving? We have stories."

Just the mention of his name made her heart skip a beat. A couple of hours of detox she could stand. An evening of talking about the man who'd just shredded her heart? Yeah.

That was not in the cards. "I'll go as long as we don't talk about Dodge at all."

"Damn, that bad, huh?" Skyler asked. "All three of those boys are idiots. Don't even get me started on Stone. Meet us out front in half an hour, and we'll still make it to The Bison's Horn before happy hour ends."

Harper sighed. Really, was going out for drinks any worse than pissed off pacing in her room? "What do I wear?"

"Yes!" Skyler let out triumphant squeal. "I knew you were our kinda woman. Drag on some jeans and a T-shirt and you'll be fine. See ya in a few."

Harper hung up the phone and looked through the open doors of her closet. Jeans she could do, but a T-shirt? She had an emerald silk sleeveless top that would have to do. It wasn't like she was going to see anyone she wanted to impress.

• • •

Wednesday nights at The Bison's Horn were a Loving brother tradition set aside for nothing—not even the deal of Dodge's career. So here he was standing at the bar, sucking down an IPA and crunching discarded peanut shells under the soles of his boots.

"You are a Class A moron, and I refuse to believe we're actually related." Griff glared at him as he downed the rest of his beer. "Even Stone's better with women than you are."

"Shut it, Griff," Dodge and Stone snarled at the same time.

Little had he realized until his brothers stole the last two barstools that this night was a May Loving matchmaking special. She'd pulled his brothers aside and spilled the whole story about him, Harper, and the universe. And to make matters worse, she'd somehow managed to finagle his brothers into acting as her matchmaking lackeys. They hadn't stopped talking about Harper since he'd tossed back his first handful of peanuts.

"You know she's leaving." Impervious to Dodge's glare, Stone just shrugged. "Skyler told me."

"Good. I'm glad she's going." He pushed against his sternum, hoping like hell that the fiery surge eating away at him was indigestion and not a heart attack. "It makes for one less distraction."

Even with the smell of beer hanging in the air, his words reeked of bullshit, and his brothers weren't the kind of men to miss that.

Griff shot him a questioning look punctuated with an all-knowing smirk. "Okay, bro. Look over your left shoulder, and tell me that again."

Dodge glanced back and nearly choked on his beer. Harper stood just inside the doorway flanked by Stone's best friend, Skyler, and the new hire in accounting, Amelia. Men's heads turned so fast to check out the trio that an ambulance-chasing lawyer would have had a field day with the whiplash cases.

He'd seen Harper dressed to the nines, totally naked, and everywhere in between, but never in ass-hugging jeans and a slip of a tank top that showed a tempting sliver of skin every time she moved. He gripped his bottle tighter so he didn't go all Neanderthal and rip every other man's eyes out so they couldn't look at Harper with the lust eating away at Dodge's sanity.

"What's wrong?" Griff drove home an elbow into Dodge's side. "Hottie got your tongue?"

Right now it felt like she had every part of him right under her spike heels, and it hurt like hell. "Like I said, I'm glad she's going."

"Fucking pathetic," Griff said.

"What makes you care so much whether Harper stays or

goes?" he asked.

"I like her," Stone said.

Griff nodded in agreement. "Anyway, having her around the past few weeks sure has made you less of an ass to live with—until now."

"Sorry to offend your delicate sensibilities, little brother."

He wasn't an ass. He was focused on The Retreat, on the Brasch Group deal, and on destroying his grandfather's company. If his brothers didn't realize that then fuck 'em.

"You should be sorry about your own behavior," Griff said as he stood up from the stool. "I'm going to hang out with the girls. I never realized that chick in accounting would look quite so good with her hair down."

Griff strutted across the bar, women practically fainting at his feet as he walked by.

"He is a harassment suit waiting to happen."

"Pretty much." Stone got up. "But he's right when it comes to your attitude. You need to cowboy up and stop hiding behind some bullshit vendetta."

Frustration spiked in Dodge's veins. "Is there anyone who doesn't think they know what's best for me?"

"Just you." Stone clinked his beer against Dodge's, then strolled over to the other side of the bar.

Stewing in his beer, Dodge sat down in his brother's vacant seat and nursed the last of his beer in bitter solitude. His brothers were as wrong as the sun setting in the east. He'd done the right thing cutting Harper out of his life. Totally. Completely. Just like—bile made his mouth bitter and his gut twisted into a complicated knot—just like his grandfather had when he'd disowned May and never looked back.

Fuck. Was he really turning into the myopic old bastard?

He watched Harper as she laughed and flirted with the men who flocked to her table. She'd never given him any reason to doubt her. He'd created false scenarios all on his own. He'd done exactly what his grandfather had done with Dodge's father. He'd acted as judge and jury without ever giving her a chance. Griff and Stone were right. He was a fucking bastard.

When Harper got up to go to the bathroom, he got up and followed without thought and without a plan. He had no clue what he was going to say, but there was no way he could let her leave like this. He had to fix everything before it was too late.

The Bison's Horn had three bathrooms—all of them unisex singles—and there was always a line, even on Wednesday night, so he wasn't surprised when he caught up with her in the hall.

Harper didn't even look his way as she stood with her arms crossed. "What do you want?"

"You." He didn't mean to say it, but the single word popped out as true a statement as he'd ever made.

At that moment, one of the bathroom doors opened. Something flashed in her chocolate-colored eyes and his cock responded with a twitch behind his zipper. Before he could take back what he'd said, Harper grabbed the untucked corner of his shirt, pulled him inside the bathroom, and slammed the door shut behind them.

Chapter Thirteen

Harper could blame the Long Island Iced Tea tomorrow morning, but tonight she wanted one last taste of the man who'd rocked her world and left her reeling from the impact—not because she couldn't stand to be without him but because she wanted to prove to herself that she could.

"What do you want?" He may have asked the question, but lust darkening his moss-green eyes said he already knew the answer.

"To fuck you and forget you." Her mouth came down on his, and her fingers flicked open the top button of his jeans.

The zipper went down in one smooth motion, and she reached inside. He was already hard for her. Hot and heavy, his cock filled her hand. She wrapped her fingers around his girth and squeezed hard enough to let him know that soft and gentle weren't in the cards tonight.

"Fast and hard with a line of people outside the door waiting to come in, huh?" He kissed his way down her neck, leaving a trail of fiery desire in his wake. "You really think you can forget me? We need to talk."

"Nothing to talk about. We're done." Anticipation licked her skin, flaming her already hot yearning to molten need. "This is just putting the cherry on the ice cream sundae of our breakup."

He wrapped his hands around her wrists, stopping her stroking motion but not pulling her away from his hard length. "Why?"

Why him? Why here? Why now? The answer was a shredded mess under her ribcage, but she wasn't going to tell him that. She could barely admit to it herself, but it was true. She'd fallen for Dodge Loving. Fallen hard and fast and, it turned out, all by herself. The only cure was to rip the bandage off and leave herself raw and aching—one last time with him would accomplish that better than anything else she could do.

Summoning up her inner bad girl who'd never seen the light of day before, she gave him a sassy wink. "It doesn't matter."

She leaned in and kissed him, her tongue sweeping across his juicy bottom lip before sweeping inside. He tasted of beer, peanuts, and bittersweet good-bye.

Dodge turned his head, cutting off the kiss. "I want to know."

She skimmed her lips with her tongue before tugging on her bottom one with her teeth, arching one eyebrow when his hold on her wrists tightened in response. Oh, he wanted her, but this time it was by her rules. "Well, for the first time in your life you're not going to get what you want."

"That's where you're wrong." He yanked her arms up as he spun her around so she faced the mirror. Then he placed her hands flat against the mirror over the small sink. "Don't move them."

Desire made her chest tight and her muscles loose. It took everything she had not to mewl in pleasure and melt into putty in his hands. But that would be giving in too soon. This last time he was going to have to work for it. So she stood rooted to the spot, her stillness a challenge for them both.

He slid a hand under the hem of her silk tank top, his palm flat against her stomach. Up or down? Whichever direction he chose, she wanted. His fingers glided up across her skin, brushing against the full bottom curve of her breast. The strength of his groan made the hair tucked behind her ear fly forward. "Christ." He pinched her nipple. "You're not wearing a bra."

"The tank's straps are too narrow." Her knees nearly buckled under his finger's blissful assault. He knew, he always knew, right where to touch her.

If only... She slapped back the thought before it could move any further into the light. Now wasn't the time and Dodge wasn't the man, no matter how much she wanted him to be.

He rolled her puckered nipple between his fingers and pushed his hardness against the cleft of her jean-covered ass. "Are you wearing panties?"

"You're going to have to find out for yourself."

Reaching around to her front, he toyed with the top button of her jeans. "I take these down, they're not coming back up until you're screaming my name loud enough for everyone in the bar to hear."

Her heart stopped beating, and all the air rushed out of her lungs when she met his gaze in the mirror. He was serious. This wasn't just talk like in her hotel room. It wasn't a tease in The Retreat's hallway. She inhaled greedily, jumpstarting her heart. The old Harper would have given in, answered. But even if she'd wanted to go back to being the woman her parents trained her to be, she couldn't. Dodge may have broken her heart, but he'd helped her figure out who she really was—her own woman.

She opened her mouth as if she was going to describe her panties, but instead she blew his reflection a kiss and watched as the vein in his temple pulsed. Then she dropped her hands to her jeans, unbuttoned them, and shimmied the denim down over her hips as far as she could with him pressed up against her from behind.

"These don't count as panties." Dodge hooked a finger around the thin black strap of her green G-string and pulled it out as far as it would go before letting the elastic snap back against her hip. "Now get your hands back up."

She did, keeping her gaze on him in the reflection. The color of her shirt nearly matched the darker hue of his eyes while his dark brown skin was the opposite of her own creamy complexion. They were so alike in some ways and completely different in others, yet they found a place in the middle where everything meshed and made sense. At least they had. The realization made her yearn for more than this one last encounter, but she squelched it before it could grow. This wasn't about more; it was about right now, because that's all they had left.

Dodge disappeared from view, dropping down and sliding her jeans and G-string down as he went until the denim was down to her ankles. His firm hands pushed her legs as wide as they would go, constrained as they were by the material, before gliding the back of his fingers up the insides of her legs as he rose up. His touch was so teasingly gentle she was panting by the time he got to the juncture of her thighs.

"So warm and wet for me." He sank a finger in and then a second, rubbing against the bundle of nerves just inside the entrance. "And it is for me."

Her eyes fluttered shut as her legs began to tremble. "Don't kill the moment with ego."

His fingers stilled, and he nipped at the sensitive spot where her shoulder and neck met. "Open your eyes and see what I see and then tell me that's just ego talking."

She did and almost climaxed from the sight. Her tank top was pushed to the side, one breast exposed. She looked like a complete hedonist. Watching his hand slide again between her thighs, rocking her closer to orgasm, the tension tightened in her belly and spread outward, making every inch of her skin tingle.

"Look at yourself. I do that to you." He increased his speed, his fingers hurtling her toward her climax. "But look at what you do to me."

Her gaze flicked up to the man behind her. Dodge stood, hard and hungry, looking every bit like a man who would take her body places she'd never been before but always wanted to go. "You make me forget about everything in the world but you."

No man should be able to look so hard and talk so sweet. Fucking him one last time had been a mistake, an emotional disaster, but she couldn't stop now. She didn't want to, no matter the consequences. He placed his palm against her lower back and tilted her forward over the sink as he withdrew his fingers from her wet folds.

"Don't stop," she said, not caring how desperate she sounded.

"You'll like this just as much." He grabbed a condom from the small bowl next to the sink and tore the foil package open with his teeth. "I promise."

He sheathed himself on the inhale and sank deep inside on her next breath, filling her completely. Locked between the hard sink and the harder man behind her, Harper gave in to the sensations washing over her, pleasure so intense it nearly blinded her. The vibrations started in her calves, zipping up her inner thighs in a race to sweet oblivion.

"Open your eyes," Dodge said against her ear. He raised his hands so they covered her hands that were still pressed against the mirror. "Watch us together."

As soon as she did, her orgasm hit and she screamed out his name. With one final deep thrust, he came with her name on his lips, his body shaking from release.

Unable to keep them open any more, she let her eyes drift shut as the aftershocks made her shiver in his arms—the one place she felt at home. Harper relaxed against Dodge, relishing the feel of his strength. She opened her eyes and blinked her surrounding slowly back into focus, and with it the real world. The bathroom. The bar. The man who'd told her in no uncertain terms to leave. Reality knocked the bliss out of her breath.

Dodge withdrew a step, and cold air swept across her overheated skin. She took advantage of the moment to pull up her pants, straighten her tank top, and calm her ragged breathing.

He disposed of the condom and buttoned his pants, guilt etching deep lines in his forehead. "About the interview..."

Her throat tightened, and she held up her hand. She stopped him before he said another word that would slice through her. "It doesn't matter."

"It does." He encircled her wrist, his touch easing and stoking her misery.

But this time she shook him off. "Maybe it matters to you, but not to me." Voice firm, her denial sounded true and, if she said that a few more times, she just might find herself believing it.

"You don't mean that. You can't after what we just did." He reached out but hesitated, his hand hovering over her skin as if he wasn't sure he had the right to touch her anymore. "It matters."

She turned her back on him and faced the mirror, studiously ignoring his reflection and hardened herself from the inside out. Might as well tell him. It's not like she had anything left to lose.

"You know, after everything, I almost went back to being the old Harper, the one who did what she was told and followed the rules and put everyone else's needs in front of her own. It wasn't until I saw you in that hallway tonight that I realized the idiocy of that path. If I ever really was that woman, I'm not anymore." She fluffed her hair and reapplied her lipstick before dropping the tube into her small purse. "It's too bad I had to fall in love with *you* to figure that out."

"Love?" It sounded like a foreign word on his tongue, new and unspoken until now.

Something twisted apart inside her, leaving a jagged hole in its place, and she knew she had to get out of there before she crumpled under the pain.

"Yes, love. But don't worry, it's not catching." She spun on her heel, crossed the small bathroom, and opened the door. "And if it was, you've got a natural immunity. Good-bye, Dodge. If you're ever in Washington, D.C., be sure not to look me up."

She strutted out of the bathroom with her head held high even as a dozen pairs of eyes watched her go. What did it matter? She'd never be back in Wyoming again.

Dodge called her name and her step faltered, regret pinching her heart, but she kept moving. Increasing her speed, she strode to the table where Skyler and Amelia sat so she could tell them she was leaving. She had to get back to The Retreat before the first tear fell.

Chapter Fourteen

Dodge carried the steaming mug of coffee out onto the family's veranda at The Retreat—not that he'd need it. Every time he closed his eyes he'd seen Harper's face as she'd told him good-bye. So he'd spent the hours since leaving The Bison's Horn pacing in his rooms and watching the sky for first light. As soon as the birds started chirping and his five a.m. alarm went off, he'd showered, pulled on a suit, and gone downstairs.

Looking out on the quiet grounds should have been a triumph. Once Jean-Luc toured The Retreat, there was no way The Brasch Group would go with Dodge's grandfather's hotels. What he'd told Harper had been true. The deal made perfect business sense. The Brasch Group wanted to create a chain of unique resorts that would fit in with each location's individual environment. His grandfather's hotel chain was all about providing a common experience where every hotel was exactly the same no matter where it was. Meshing The Brasch Group's vision with his grandfather's hotel made about as much sense as Harper last night. None at all. And because he wouldn't be touching her soft skin, or hearing her lusty moans, or watching her come apart in his arms again, he'd concentrate on the one thing he could do something about—closing this deal.

Garth Hampton emerged from behind a trio of trees, slowed his pace, and jogged toward the veranda. Finally, something was going Dodge's way. He'd been trying to track down the rock star for the past day to find out what he could do to make up for the photo going viral.

Hair slicked back into a man bun and in a worn SEX & DRUGS & ROCK-N-ROLL T-shirt soaked through with sweat, Garth stopped in front of the veranda's steps, gulping in lungsful of air. Dodge grabbed one of the oversized bottles of water his mom kept in a decorative cooler and handed it to the other man.

"Thanks." Garth pressed the cool bottle to the back of his flushed neck. "You look like you ran over your own dog."

Didn't he know it. "Mr. Hampton, I'd like to apologize."

"Did you run over *my* dog?"

Dodge laughed despite himself. "No."

Garth cocked his head. "Then I can't imagine why you need to apologize to me."

Dodge set down his coffee on one of the small tables scattered across the veranda and rubbed the back of his neck, his muscles a tense line from his head to his shoulders. "For the photos and the reporters and the general mishandling of your stay here. We'll of course give you a full refund and find new lodgings."

Garth snorted. "I'm not going anywhere, and I have a lot more money to spend now that it's not going up my nose, so I might as well spend it here." He twisted open the bottle of water and took a long drink. "I've spent decades in the public eye. Paparazzi have tracked me down in club bathrooms, at my dealer's house, and even once on a yacht in the middle of the Gulf of Mexico. The fact that you kept them off the scent for as long as you did is pretty much a miracle."

He hadn't thought about it that way. For him, keeping the press away was another zero-sum game. He either won it all or lost it all with no in between. "If you're sure…"

"I am." Garth gave Dodge an assessing look as he chugged down the rest of the water. "But you still look like shit. Late night or a woman?"

The question was a hard backhand against his cheek, and it hurt enough to make his teeth ache. "Both."

"Deadly combination that." Garth sat down on The Retreat's front steps and slapped the empty spot beside him. "Tell me the story, and we'll call ourselves even for the lying reporters snapping pictures of me. Holding a vodka bottle my ass. You know that was a water bottle, right?"

Dodge hesitated. He wasn't a talk-it-out kind of guy and especially not to a guest. "I don't think—"

"Do you know how many recovery meetings I've sat through?" Garth narrowed his eyes and smacked the wood step beside him again. "Enough to know there is nothing in the world you can say that will shock or surprise me. Sit down and let it out."

Maybe it was the exhaustion, or the aching feeling that he'd fucked up in a way that couldn't be fixed, but Dodge sat down, stared out at the landscape turned golden by the dawn's light, and spilled his guts. He told Garth the whole story starting with his plan for revenge by ruining his grandfather's hotel business and ending with Harper walking away from him at The Bison's Horn. "I couldn't sleep. So I paced my room until it was late enough that I could go to my office and start prepping for The Brasch Group representatives' tour."

His office. It was the last place he wanted to be, but the only place he was welcome—Harper had made that more than clear.

"Man." Garth shook his head. "You didn't ask me for advice, and God knows I'm not an authority on happily ever after, but you need to get that girl to stay. Man, you need to get down on your knees and grovel."

His gut cramped. Garth may be right, but there wasn't a damn thing Dodge could do about it. Harper had been more than clear last night. She was right—this time he wasn't going to get his way, because letting her have her way was more important. At this point, it was the only thing he could offer her.

The aging rocker stood and walked down the steps where he paused and turned back to Dodge. "If you don't, you'll regret it, and I *am* an expert in regrets."

Garth's life story was the stuff of legends. He'd vaulted to superstardom decades ago and had never fallen. Critics loved him, fans adored him, and groupies had flocked to him. Yet, he still ended up losing himself in drugs and alcohol. Regrets. Yeah, they both had a few.

"Why The Retreat?" Dodge couldn't help but ask. "You could be on an island in the middle of nowhere without any threat of paparazzi."

"You're not the only one with a master plan." Garth winked and took off at a jog down the path to his private cabin.

• • •

It was close to seven by the time Dodge carried his now lukewarm cup of coffee into his office where he found the last person he expected to see there: his mother. May made it a point not to be involved in the day-to-day operations at The Retreat, but here she was sitting behind his desk, flipping through the folder marked The Brasch Group.

His mom in his office meant trouble of the matchmaking

momma kind, exactly what he didn't need right now if he was going to finally give Harper what she wanted, what she deserved.

"You're up early," he said.

May rose from his chair and walked around to the front of the desk. She took his face between her palms and looked hard at the bags under his eyes and probably all the way down to the weariness of his soul.

She tsk-tsked. "At least I went to sleep. It looks like you didn't even catch a wink."

Stepping out of her grasp, he walked to the other side of the desk and half flopped down into his chair. "What can I help you with?"

May sat in the guest chair across from him, crossed her legs into lotus pose, and rested the back of her hands on her knees before taking in a deep breath and letting it out slowly. "You can help me with Harper."

Just hearing her name out loud hurt. He scrubbed his hand over his face, as if he could wash away the past twenty-four hours, but he couldn't. It was too late. "Mom, this isn't the time for your matchmaking games."

She lost a little bit of her Zen sheen, and her eyes narrowed. "Okay, then let's talk about you and your foolhardy quest to ruin your own grandfather."

He'd spent the past year setting up this deal, wooing the investors, and watching the man who'd disowned his own daughter without a second thought get closer and closer to the edge of financial ruin. It wasn't just revenge; it was retribution. "He deserves it."

"That may be so," May said. "But getting your own hands dirty like this only leaves you with muck under your fingernails. Trust me, the last thing you want to do is be so hell-bent on beating your grandfather that you turn into him."

"It's too late."

"Oh, honey. It's never too late. The universe is always moving, always changing, and you can, too."

Didn't he wish. But with Harper gone, what was the point?

"I have to close this deal." Of all the people in his family, he knew she'd be the hardest sell, but deep down she had to understand. "The deal is all I have left to redeem myself."

"Why?" She uncrossed her legs and jumped up from her seat in one fluid motion. "Because your grandfather was an idiot before you were even born?"

Born. That was the problem, wasn't it? Heat blasted his face, and his hands tightened into fists. "Did you ever think if it hadn't been for me, he would have reacted differently?"

May planted her palms on his desk, her whole body trembling. Anger, frustration, sadness—they all came off her in waves, but when he looked up into his mother's eyes all he saw was love.

"Your grandfather didn't disown me because I was pregnant with you." Her lips curled in a sad smile. "He did it because your father was black, and I'd broken some unwritten code that existed only in his mind. None of it is your fault. You're not responsible for your grandfather's pigheaded reactions."

"But he should pay for what he did." He was as certain about that as he was that the sun would rise in the east and that beer tasted best on Saturday afternoons in September while watching college football.

May shook her head as she sank back into the guest chair. "You don't need to redeem yourself, Dodge. Not to me, not to your father. All this obsession with revenge only blocks you from seeing what's right in front of you."

But that was the catch, wasn't it? Harper didn't want to be right in front of him. She wanted to be half a country away—and after the way he'd acted the other day, he couldn't fault her for wanting to put 2,076 miles between them.

"She's leaving today."

He didn't need the reminder. All he could think about was the totally neutral look on her face when she'd told him good-bye, like she'd already forgotten him. "I know, I'm the asshole who told her to go."

"And have you asked her to stay?" May slapped her palms against the chair's arms, her voice uncharacteristically loud and strident. "Have you fought for her with as much effort as you've put into this plan of yours with The Brasch Group?"

"What difference would it make?" he yelled, his heart hammering against his chest like it was going to make a break for it and chase after Harper. "She's made up her mind."

His phone rang, startling them both into silence. He yanked the receiver free. "Hello?"

"Mr. Loving, this is Paul from the front gate. The Brasch Group representatives are coming up the drive now."

His gaze jerked to the clock on the wall. It wasn't even eight o'clock. "They weren't supposed to be here until ten."

"Well, they're early."

"Thank you, Paul." He hung up. It had taken all his powers of persuasion to get Jean-Luc to agree to come to The Retreat. There was no way he'd get this close to making the deal of his life, and he wasn't going to fuck it up now, especially not to beat his head against the brick wall of Harper's decision. He stood and straightened his tie. "I gotta go, Mom."

Not giving her time to stop him, he hustled to the door and opened it, mentally preparing for whatever this tour held.

"Dodge," his mother called out. "Imagine your life without her. That's what's at stake here."

His step faltered, but he powered on. Harper had made her decision. It was too late now.

• • •

More of a surprise inspection than a formality-only tour, Dodge led Jean-Luc and his three-man team around the hotel. They started in the behind the scenes areas like the kitchen.

"And this is the walk-in freezer." Dodge opened the door as he was pelted with images of Harper sitting on the prep table in her form-fitting yoga pants, laughing while stealing bites of his ice cream. He could still taste the chocolate mint on her lips and the whipped cream left behind on the corner of her mouth. An ache began in his chest, spreading outward until he hurt right down to the marrow in his bones.

Jean-Luc looked around the walk-in. "You have a lot of small pints of ice cream."

He'd ordered enough for six months with at least three pints in every flavor. The kitchen staff had thought he was nuts. He probably was. "We have a guest partial to midnight snacking."

Jean-Luc looked at him, his eyes wide with shock. "And he or she is allowed free reign in the kitchen?"

"She's a very special guest." Smart. Sexy. Tempting as hell. Special didn't even begin to describe Harper.

The Frenchman gave him a considering look. "I see."

Unwilling to find out exactly what it was that Jean-Luc saw, Dodge kept the tour moving. Next it was the upstairs guest rooms. A bellboy stood outside of the honeymoon suite, an empty luggage cart at the ready.

"What is this?" Jean-Luc asked.

Dodge nodded at the employee to answer, not trusting his own voice to stay neutral when Harper was on the other side of that door getting ready to leave forever.

"Ms. Conner isn't quite done packing yet," the bellboy responded.

"Ah, the fascinating Ms. Conner. I read about her in the paper," Jean-Luc said. "Things will quiet down quite a bit with her leaving, no?"

Bitterness coated his mouth. Quiet? Like an empty tomb.

"They will." Dodge shoved his hands in his pockets before he gave in to the urge to open Harper's door and stop her from going. "Has the front desk arranged for transportation to the airport?"

"No. Mrs. Loving offered The Retreat's limo. They're going to take the back way to the airport so as to not alert the paparazzi."

It would add an extra half hour to the trip, but it would be worth it to protect her from the media. She'd already sacrificed her privacy once for him, and he was glad she wouldn't have to do it a second time.

"Your team thinks of everything, it seems," Jean-Luc said.

"We try." But had he?

Ignoring the regret weighing down his steps, he continued forward. Always forward. It was a quick trip through the common guest areas such as the lobby, restaurant, and wine bar before they ended up on the front porch. A pair of horses were tied to the hitching post at the east end and The Retreat's long black limousine with its dark tinted windows idled in the drive. Garth Hampton, cleaned up after his morning run, chatted with the driver as they stood next to the limo.

He wanted to slit the limo's tires. Tie the driver up and stuff him in the trunk. Run up the stairs and beg Harper to stay. But none of that was possible. He'd fucked up the whole situation too badly to fix it now. So he swallowed past the pain squeezing his throat closed and concentrated on what he could fix—this deal.

"If you don't mind waiting, I can arrange for a golf cart to be brought around for a tour of the grounds," he told Jean-

Luc.

"That won't be necessary. I've seen everything I needed to." He turned and smiled. "Let's go sign the paperwork."

The elation Dodge had expected at the news never arrived. It was the biggest moment of his life, and he didn't give a shit. Ten minutes later he sat at a table in the small conference room overlooking the driveway with Jean-Luc, each man holding a Montblanc pen. The paperwork, the details of which had been negotiated by lawyers weeks ago, sat in a stack in front of Dodge. All he had to do was sign, and everything he'd been working toward would be realized. His grandfather's hotels would fail and The Retreat would become a global home for luxury.

His phone vibrated on the table with an incoming text.

Mom: They're loading her bags.

Although not unexpected, it was still a gut punch that knocked the wind out of him. Grinding his teeth together, he replaced the phone on the table with exacting care. His phone vibrated again.

Mom: There's still time.

He wished that were true, but he knew the truth even if his matchmaking mother did not. His phone vibrated again. This time he turned it off without looking at the message.

"It's not another press invasion, is it?" Jean-Luc nodded toward Dodge's phone.

"Not even close." He held the pen so tight its metal clip bit into his palm.

Jean-Luc sat back and tapped his pen against his chin. "But something you have to take care of?"

"No, I—" Movement in the large window caught his attention. The limo turned slowly out of the driveway. Dodge's heart stopped, and the entire world fell away. All he could see was Harper. Her red hair twisting in the air churned up by the helicopter. The pink flush that covered her pale skin when she laughed hard. The way she'd looked when she slept, soft and sexy, the most beautiful person he'd ever seen. And if he didn't get out of here now, he'd never see her again. He had one chance, and he wasn't going to lose it. His heart whammed back to life in his chest. "I have to go."

He was halfway to the door before Jean-Luc's voice stopped him.

"And if I were to say that if you leave now we make the deal with your grandfather's hotels?"

Dodge waited for the familiar fury at his grandfather to well up, but it didn't. The only thing that mattered was getting to Harper. "Then I'd wish you luck, but you know it's the wrong move."

"Am I right to assume you are chasing after Ms. Conner?"

"You are." He barely paused in the doorway to acknowledge the other man's question.

"Then you better hurry." Jean-Luc chuckled. "Don't be so shocked. I am French, after all; romance and drama are our national pastimes. Go, we will sign the papers tomorrow."

Dodge rushed down the hall, swerving around wide-eyed guests and shocked maids until he burst out of The Retreat's front doors. Off in the distance he could see the small cloud of dust kicked up by the limo's tires as it took the dirt back road. There was still time. Frantic, he searched for a car or golf cart, but the driveway was empty, except for a fully saddled Appaloosa stallion tied to the hitching post.

Chapter Fifteen

Harper could have walked to the airport faster than the limo driver drove. It wasn't because of traffic; there wasn't any. No, she had the one driver in the world who believed in driving ten miles *under* the thirty-five miles per hour speed limit on the winding dirt road leading to the airport. He'd promised it was a shortcut to the airport compared to the paved highway and, like an idiot, she'd agreed. Sinking lower in her seat, she closed her eyes, hoping to block out the last bits of Wyoming landscape she'd ever see.

It didn't help. Without the scenery to distract her, all she could see was Dodge. The look in his eyes any time she'd touched him. The way he'd smiled when she realized he'd set up the surprise picnic on Sandpiper Island. The way he took her breath away every time he said her name. She bit down on her quaking lip.

She couldn't get to the airport fast enough. Dodge didn't really care about her. For him, it was all about The Retreat. He didn't have room in his life for anything or anyone else, and she refused to fall back into her old habits of only being a means for someone else to reach success. Leaving was the right thing to do, but that didn't make it hurt any less.

The tinted window separating the back of the limo from the driver rolled down.

"Now that's something you don't get a gander at every day." The driver tapped on the brakes. "There's a man on a horse chasing us."

Adrenaline spiked in her veins. She jerked upright in her seat and spun around to look out the back window. There was a horse and rider coming after them hell-bent for leather. She squinted. And that rider was Dodge.

The limo slowed even more.

Her pulse went into overdrive. It was ridiculous. She pinched her cheeks to put a little color back into them. It was idiotic. She couldn't help but smile. It was absolutely marvelous. Harper tightened her grip on her purse to keep herself from flinging open the door. Even as the giddy, fizzy feeling threatened to take over, she had to stay strong. She'd forgiven him too many times already. She wasn't sure she could take Dodge breaking her heart again. Turning away from the back window, she promised herself she wouldn't look back.

"Hit the gas." Her request sounded pathetic even to her own ears.

"But he'll never catch us if I speed up," the driver said.

Unable to stop herself, she twisted in her seat so she could look out the back window. Her heart contracted. Dodge had gained on them, his horse galloping at full speed and Dodge's navy suit jacket flapping in the wind.

"He looks ludicrous riding a horse in a three-piece suit." She sniffled and bit the inside of her cheek.

"Definitely a fool," the driver said. "A fool in love."

Despite knowing better, she couldn't help but root for him to catch up before the turnoff for the highway. As if hearing her thoughts instead of her words, the limo driver steered the vehicle over to the side of the dirt road and turned off the engine.

Harper whipped her head around in surprise. "Why did you stop?"

The driver turned around and took off his sunglasses and chauffeur's hat. Long hair tumbled down, and he gave her a grin that had been mesmerizing stadiums full of people for thirty years. She gasped in shock. What in the hell was Garth Hampton doing driving the limo?

"What..."

He laughed. "Let's just say that the real driver is a fan who was more than happy to swap clothes with me. I had a long talk with your fella this morning and I figured he just might change his mind about coming after you."

It didn't make any sense. "But why?"

"Like I said..." Garth shrugged and nodded toward the back window. "He's a fool in love."

She turned around in time to see Dodge rein his horse to a stop next to the limo. Her heart hammered against her ribs. She eyeballed the door locks. There was still time, but she couldn't do it. When it came to Dodge, her heart always won out.

He dismounted and yanked open the door.

• • •

Dodge hadn't thought past halting the limo, but his mouth wasn't going to let that stop him. "Don't go."

Harper got out of the limo, fire in her eyes, and slammed the door shut behind her. "What in the hell do you think you're doing?"

For the first time in his life, he had no idea. "Whatever it takes to make you stay. I'm an idiot and I'm sorry. You tried to help—no, you did help and, instead of seeing that, all I could do was think about how it would affect the deal to take The Retreat global. I'd been so focused on making my grandfather pay for so long that I couldn't see that it was turning me into a real bastard just like him."

She cocked her head to the side and gave him a considering look that went from the dumbass lovestruck face to the Wyoming dust covering every single inch of him. He didn't look like much of a reason to stay, but he had to hope she'd see through that.

"You're forgiven." Her tone said he was anything but. "Now if you'll—"

Harper reached for the door handle, but Dodge pivoted so his shoulder was against the door. She could try, but that door wasn't opening until he was done. She crossed her arms and sighed but didn't slam a heel down on his instep to get him to move. That was progress.

He reached out and tucked a stray red lock behind her ear. Her breath hitched. His fingers lingered on her lobe before tracing a line across her jaw. Touching her was a risk, but he couldn't help himself. When he was around Harper he lost focus on anything but her. Anyway, if he lost her, he didn't have anything else to risk. This was the ultimate all or nothing situation and he was putting it all on the line.

"The worst part is..." He looked into her eyes, hating himself for the hurt he saw in them. "I was so obsessed that I lashed out at the one person who only wanted to help." He stepped closer and tilted her chin upward, praying this wouldn't be the last time he touched her. "The one woman I love."

She blinked the moisture out of her eyes and exhaled a shaky breath. "Love?"

"Yes. Love." He brushed his lips across hers, desperate for more but knowing he had to tell her everything first. "I love the way you light up every room you walk into. I love that you turn on my brain and my body every time I'm near you. I love that you add whipped cream to your whipped cream on your ice cream sundaes. I love the way you make everything better just by being yourself. You don't have to change who you are into some new version of Harper or back to the woman you were before. You are perfect just the way you are."

She stared at him, her mouth firmly shut. The only sound Dodge could hear was the blood rushing in his ears as his lungs burned from the breath he was holding.

Then...she smiled. "That's a lot of words."

Relief rushed through him and he gathered her in his arms. "And I mean every single one of them."

"You broke my heart."

And he'd spend the next six decades making up for it. "It'll never happen again. I love you, Harper Conner."

She raised herself up to her tiptoes, her lips only millimeters from his. "I love you, too."

It wasn't their first kiss and it wouldn't be their last, but Dodge put everything he had into it, every promise he'd yet to make, and every commitment he'd keep. The universe might be laughing its ass off at him, but he couldn't care less. He had the woman he loved, and that's all that mattered.

The limo's driver side window rolled down, and Garth poked his head out. "I do believe that's my cue to exit. Did you want me to take you back to The Retreat?"

Dodge looked down at Harper. With her hair flying in the Wyoming wind and her kiss-swollen lips, she gave him the best idea. There was a blanket roll attached to the Appaloosa's saddle, perfect for a little outdoor adventure. He nodded his chin at the blanket. Harper's eyes grew wide with understanding before her eyelids drooped down slightly and she sucked on her bottom lip. The sight made his cock twitch.

"Thanks, Garth, but I've got it covered." Dodge took off his suit jacket and vest, then threw them into the limo's backseat before turning to Harper.

A few minutes later they were both on the Appaloosa and the limo was half a mile down the road. Harper's skirt was hiked up to mid-thigh so she could sit in the saddle, and the soft globes of her ass were nestled up against the growing bulge behind his zipper.

"So what's next?" She wiggled her butt like she had no idea what her movements were doing to him.

He kissed the soft spot at the base of her neck. "Now we ride into the sunset."

She glanced up at the bright blue sky. "You realize it's eleven in the morning."

He laughed and flicked the reins, signaling the Appaloosa to start moving. "I can call back the limo."

She relaxed against him as they moved across the open field. "But then you'd only have to chase me down again."

"And I would." He clicked his tongue against the back of his teeth, and the horse picked up the pace. They needed to get to the secret spot down by river sooner rather than later.

Harper twisted and looked up at him. "Always?"

Dodge tried to imagine his life without her and he couldn't and, quite frankly, he never wanted to. "Always."

Chapter Sixteen

Harper stood next to Dodge as he sat in his office chair.

The seating chart for their wedding had been pushed aside for a hurriedly sketched out three-month calendar. They'd been talking about dates, but all that had tapered off as soon as he'd slipped one hand under her knee-length skirt. Heart pounding, she watched the door, knowing that his large desk blocked what they were doing...or might be doing in a second...from view. Her breath caught when his fingers glided another half inch up her inner thigh. He kept talking about likely dates and listing pros and cons, but all she could think about was how much longer it would take him to walk his fingers up from the inside of her thigh to where she really wanted him to be. Another half inch up. She bit down on her lip, the anticipation swirling in her stomach, and her eyes drifted shut so she could concentrate more on the tingling sensation in her core.

A sharp *rap* sounded at the door. She snapped her eyes

open, and Dodge removed his teasing fingers from her leg. Griff sauntered in, Stone a step behind.

"What's up?" Griff asked.

"We're putting together an office pool," Harper blurted out as she hurried away from the desk and the temptation Dodge offered.

Stone cocked an eyebrow. "For what?"

"To see which one of you two is up next and when you go down." Dodge's voice dripped with the kind of glee that only came with tormenting younger brothers.

It had taken her a few weeks, but once she realized the Loving brothers communicated via snark and expressed love by giving each other shit, their close relationship began to make sense.

"No," Stone and Griff said at the same time.

"My money's on Stone." Harper slapped a five-dollar bill onto the table by the office door.

Dodge got up, removing his wallet as he walked over to her, took out his wallet and withdrew a five. "I'll take that bet because I'm going with Griff. Mom likes a challenge." He dropped his money next to hers.

Standing so close to him made her pulse tick faster, reminding her exactly of what had been about to happen before his brothers knocked on the door. "And you don't think you were enough of a challenge?"

"When it comes to finding the perfect match for these two?" He nodded his chin at his brothers. "I was just the warm-up act."

The brothers looked at each other, both wearing identical expressions of horror and fear.

"I'm telling her I found the perfect girl for you," Stone said.

"Not if I get to her first," Griff replied.

Stone and Griff scrambled out of Dodge's office fast

enough that she would have laughed if her attention hadn't already gone back to the man who had stolen far more than just her focus. Dodge Loving had stolen her heart.

"A warm-up act, huh?" She shut his office door. "So what do you do for the main event?"

Desire swirled in his eyes, and he dropped his gaze to her mouth before reaching around her and locking his office door. "Let me show you."

And he did.

Acknowledgments

Wyoming? Who would have ever thought I'd write a book set in Wyoming? Not me, that's for sure. But still Dodge, Stone, and Griff popped into my head while I was hunkered down in a hotel with three kids, two dogs, and one sleeping husband while a bazillion feet of snow fell outside—and now the Loving brothers are here for you. I hope you enjoy them. I couldn't have made Dodging Temptation happen without the help of some amazing people, including my editor Alethea Spiridon Hopson (who I'm sure is laughing her Canadian self silly at the idea of a bazillion feet of snow in Virginia) and the rest of the team at Entangled—including Nancy C. who is a copyediting genius.

Happy reading!

Xoxo,

Avery

About the Author

When Avery Flynn isn't writing about alpha heroes and the women who tame them, she is desperately hoping someone invents the coffee IV drip. She has three slightly wild children, loves a hockey-addicted husband, and has a slight shoe addiction. Find out more about Avery on her website, follow her on Twitter, like her Facebook page or friend her Facebook profile. Also, if you figure out how to send Oreos through the internet, she'll be your best friend for life. Contact her at avery@averyflynn.com. She'd love to hear from you.

Discover more category romance titles from Entangled Indulgence...

GIVING UP THE BOSS
a *Billionaire's Second Chance* novel by Victoria Davies

Billionaire Jackson Sinclair wakes up in a hospital to a life he can't remember. The only person who feels familiar is Lori. The more he learns about his past, though, the more it disturbs him. He can't imagine why the lovely Lori put up with him. And she is lovely, as in, he can't stop thinking about her. But he has a company to save, and there's no time for that sort thing. Especially when it seems like his assistant is hiding something from him.

THE PENTHOUSE PRINCE
a novel by Virginia Nelson

Single mom Jeanie Long was trying to save her butt at work by reporting her manager to the company owner. Instead, she finds herself greeted warmly by gorgeous company CEO Camden James, and introduced to his father as his fiancée. Now she's been hired—complete with a hefty pay raise—to be Camden's fake fiancée. Except that their "for the press" kisses look incredibly *real*. Which means Jeanie and Camden are very convincing actors...or they've fallen for their own charade.

BEAUTY AND THE BACHELOR
a *Bachelor Auction* novel by Naima Simone

Billionaire Lucas Oliver is hell bent on revenge. And his plan begins when Sydney Blake—the stunning daughter of his enemy—is tricked into bidding on Lucas at a bachelor auction. Then he serves up a little blackmail...followed by a marriage proposal Sydney has no choice but to accept. Now she's engaged to a darkly handsome beast intent on destroying her entire family...along with her heart.